A KNOT
IN THE
GRAIN
AND
OTHER
STORIES

**Other Books
by Robin McKinley
Available from
HarperTrophy**

———

BEAUTY

ROBIN McKINLEY

A KNOT IN THE GRAIN

AND OTHER STORIES

HarperTrophy
A Division of HarperCollinsPublishers

"The Healer" first appeared in *Elsewhere*, Volume II, edited by Terri Windling and Mark Alan Arnold, published in 1982 by Ace Books.

"The Stagman" first appeared in *Elsewhere* Volume III, edited by Terri Windling and Mark Alan Arnold, published in 1984 by Ace Fantasy Books/The Berkley Publishing Group.

"Touk's House" first appeared in *Faery!*, edited by Terry Windling, published in 1985 by Ace Fantasy Books/The Berkley Publishing Group.

For information address HarperCollins Children's Books, a division of
HarperCollins Publishers, 10 East 53rd Street, New York, NY 10022.
Published by arrangement with Greenwillow Books,
a division of William Morrow & Company, Inc.
LC Number 93-17557
Trophy ISBN 0-06-440604-0
First Harper Trophy edition, 1995.

TO

Mary Lou,

who brought me to

Cumberland Lodge

Contents

The Healer 1

The Stagman 41

Touk's House 73

Buttercups 107

A Knot in the Grain 149

A KNOT
IN THE
GRAIN
AND
OTHER
STORIES

The Healer

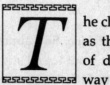**T**he child was born just as the first faint rays of dawn made their way through the cracks between the shutters. The lantern-wick burned low. The new father bowed his head over his wife's hand as the midwife smiled at the mite of humanity in her arms. Black curls framed the tiny face; the child gave a gasp of shock, then filled its lungs for its first cry in this world; but when the little mouth opened, no sound came out. The midwife tightened her hands on the warm wet skin as the baby gave a sudden writhe, and closed its mouth as if it knew that it had failed at something expected of it. Then the eyes stared up into the midwife's own, black, and clearer than a new-born's should be, and deep in them such a look of sorrow that tears rose in the midwife's own eyes.

"The child does not cry," the mother whispered in terror, and the father's head snapped up to look at the midwife and the baby cradled in her arms.

The midwife could not fear the sadness in this baby's eyes; and she said shakily, "No, the baby does not cry, but she is a fine girl nonetheless"; and the baby blinked, and the look was gone. The midwife washed her quickly, and gave her into her mother's eager, anxious arms, and saw the damp-curled, black-haired head of the young wife bend over the tiny curly head of the daughter. Her smile reminded the midwife of the smiles of many other new mothers, and the midwife smiled herself, and opened a shutter long enough to take a few deep breaths of the new morning air. She closed it again firmly, and chased the father out of the room so that mother and child might be bathed properly, and the bedclothes changed.

They named her Lily. She almost never cried; it was as though she did not want to call attention to what she lacked, and so at most her little face would screw itself into a tiny red knot, and a few tears would creep down her cheeks; but she did not open her mouth. She was her parents' first child, and her mother hovered over her, and she suffered no neglect for her inability to draw attention to herself.

When Lily was three years old, her mother bore a second child, another daughter; when she was six and a half, a son was born. Both these children came into the world howling mightily. Lily seemed to find their wordless crying more fascinating than the grown-ups' speech, and when she could she loved to sit beside the new baby and play with it gently, and make it chuckle at her.

By the time her little brother was taking his first wobbly steps it had become apparent that Lily had been granted the healer's gift. A young cow or skittish mare would foal more quietly with her head in Lily's lap; children with fever did not toss and turn in their beds if Lily sat beside them; and it was usually in Lily's presence that the fevers broke, and the way back to health began.

When she was twelve, she was apprenticed to the midwife who had birthed her.

Jolin by then was a strong handsome woman of forty-five or so. Her husband had died when they had had only two years together, and no children; and she had decided that she preferred to live alone as a healer after that. But it was as the midwife she was best known, for her village was a healthy one; hardly anyone ever fell from a horse and broke a leg or caught a fever that her odd-smelling draughts could not bring down.

"I'll tell you, young one," she said to Lily, "I'll teach you everything I know, but if you stay here you won't be needing it; you'll spend the time you're not birthing babies sewing little sacks of herbs for the women to hang in the wardrobes and tuck among the linens. Can you sew properly?" Lily nodded, smiling; but Jolin looked into her black eyes and saw the same sorrow there that she had first seen twelve years ago. She said abruptly, "I've heard you whistling. You can whistle more like the birds than the birds do. There's no reason you can't talk with those calls; we'll put meanings to the different ones, and we'll both learn 'em. Will you do that with me?"

Lily nodded eagerly, but her smile broke, and Jolin looked away.

Five years passed; Jolin had bought her apprentice a horse the year before, because Lily's fame had begun to spread to neighboring towns, and she often rode a long way to tend the sick. Jolin still birthed babies, but she was happy not to have to tend stomachaches at midnight anymore, and Lily was nearly a woman grown, and had surpassed her old teacher in almost all Jolin had to offer her. Jolin was glad of it, for it still worried her that the sadness stayed deep in Lily's eyes and would not be lost or buried. The work meant much to each of them; for Jolin it had eased the loss of a husband she loved, and had had for so little time she could not quite let go of his memory; and for Lily, now, she thought it meant that which she had never had.

Of the two of them, Jolin thought, Lily was the more to be pitied. Their village was one of a number of small villages, going about their small concerns, uninterested in anything but the weather and the crops, marriages, births, and deaths. There was no one within three days' ride who could read or write, for Jolin knew everyone; and the birdcall-speech that she and her apprentice had made was enough for crops and weather, births and deaths, but Jolin saw other things passing swiftly over Lily's clear face, and wished there were a way to let them free.

At first Jolin had always accompanied Lily on her rounds, but as Lily grew surer of her craft, somehow she also grew able to draw what she needed to know or to borrow from whomever she tended; and Jolin could sit at home and sew her little sacks of herbs and prepare the infusions Lily would need, and tend the several cats that always lived with them, and the goats in the shed and the few chickens in the coop that survived the local foxes.

When Lily was seventeen, Jolin said, "You should be thinking of marrying." She knew at least two lads who followed Lily with their eyes and were clumsy at their work when she was near, though Lily seemed unaware of them.

Lily frowned and shook her head.

"Why not?" Jolin said. "You can be a healer as well. I was. It takes a certain kind of man"—she sighed—"but there are a few. What about young Armar? He's a quiet, even-handed sort, who'd be proud to have a wife that was needed by half the countryside. I've seen him watching you." She chuckled. "And I have my heart set on birthing your first baby."

Lily shook her head more violently, and raised her hands to her throat.

"You can learn to whistle at him as you have me," Jolin said gently, for she saw how the girl's hands shook. "Truly, child, it's not that great a matter; five villages love you and not a person in 'em cares you can't talk."

Lily stood up, her eyes full of the bitter fire in her heart, and struck herself on the breast with her fist, and Jolin winced at the weight of the blow; she did not need to hear the words to know that Lily was shouting at her: *I do!*

Lily reached her twentieth year unmarried, although she had had three offers, Armar among them. The crop of children in her parents' home had reached seven since she had left them eight years ago; and all her little brothers and sisters whistled birdcalls at her when she whistled to them. Her mother called her children her flock of starlings; but the birds themselves would come and perch on Lily's outstretched fingers, and on no one else's.

Lily was riding home from a sprained ankle in a neighboring village, thinking about supper, and wondering if Karla had had her kittens yet when she realized she was overtaking another traveller on the road. She did not recognize the horse, and reined back her own, for she dreaded any contact with strangers; but the rider had already heard her approach and was waiting for her. Reluctantly she rode forward. The rider threw back the hood of his cloak as she approached and smiled at her. She had never seen him before; he had a long narrow face, made longer by lines of sorrow around his mouth. His long hair was blond and grey mixed, and he sat his horse as if he had been sitting on horseback for more years past than he would wish to remember. His eyes were pale, but in the fading twilight she could not see if they were blue or grey.

"Pardon me, lady," he greeted her, "but I fear I have come wrong somewhere. Would you have the goodness to tell me where I am?"

She shook her head, looking down at the long quiet hands holding his horse's reins, then forced herself to look up, meeting his eyes. She watched his face for comprehension as she shook her head again, and touched two fingers to her mouth and her throat; and said sadly to herself, *I cannot tell you anything, stranger. I cannot talk.*

The stranger's expression changed indeed, but the comprehension she expected was mixed with something else she could not name. Then she heard his words clearly in her mind, although he did not move his lips. *Indeed, but I can hear you, lady.*

Lily reached out, not knowing that she did so, and her fingers closed on a fold of the man's cloak. He did not flinch from her touch, and her horse stood patiently still, wanting its warm stall and its oats, but too polite to protest. *Who— who are you?* she thought frantically. *What are you doing to me?*

Be easy, lady. I am—here there was an odd flicker—*a mage, of sorts; or once I was one. I retain a few powers. I*—and his thought went suddenly blank with an emptiness that was much more awful than that of a voice fallen silent—*I can mindspeak. You have not met any of . . . us . . . before?*

She shook her head.

There are not many. He looked down into the white face that

8

looked up at him and felt an odd creaky sensation where once he might have had a heart.

Where are you going? she said at last.

He looked away; she thought he stared at the horizon as if he expected to see something he could hastily describe as his goal.

I do not mean to question you, she said; *forgive me, I am not accustomed to . . . speech . . . and I forget my manners.*

He smiled at her, but the sad lines around his mouth did not change. *There is no lack of courtesy*, he replied; *only that I am a wanderer, and I cannot tell you where I am going.* He looked up again, but there was no urgency in his gaze this time. *I have not travelled here before, however, and even a . . . wanderer . . . has his pride; and so I asked you the name of this place.*

She blushed that she had forgotten his question, and replied quickly, the words leaping into her mind. *The village where I live lies just there, over the little hill. Its name is Rhungill. That way*—she turned in her saddle—*is Teskip, where I am returning from; this highway misses it, it lay to your right, beyond the little forest as you rode this way.*

He nodded gravely. *You have always lived in Rhungill?*

She nodded; the gesture felt familiar, but a bubble of joy beat in her throat that she need not halt with the nod. *I am the apprentice of our healer.*

He was not expecting to hear himself say: *Is there an inn in your village, where a wanderer might rest for the night?* In the private part of his mind he said to himself: There are three hours till sunset; there is no reason to stop here now. If there are no more villages, I have lain by a fire under a tree more often than I have lain in a bed under a roof for many years past.

Lily frowned a moment and said, *No-o, we have no inn;*

Rhungill is very small. But there is a spare room—it is Jolin's house, but I live there too—we often put people up, who are passing through and need a place to stay. The villagers often send us folk. And because she was not accustomed to mindspeech, he heard her say to herself what she did not mean for him to hear: *Let him stay a little longer.*

And so he was less surprised when he heard himself answer: *I would be pleased to spend the night at your healer's house.*

A smile, such as had never before been there, bloomed on Lily's face; her thoughts tumbled over one another and politely he did not listen, or let her know that he might have. She let her patient horse go on again, and the stranger's horse walked beside.

They did not speak. Lily found that there were so many things she would like to say, to ask, that they overwhelmed her; and then a terrible shyness closed over her, for fear that she would offend the stranger with her eagerness, with the rush of pent-up longing for the particulars of conversation. He held his silence as well, but his reasons stretched back over many wandering years, although once or twice he did look in secret at the bright young face beside him, and again there was the odd, uncomfortable spasm beneath his breastbone.

They rode over the hill and took a narrow, well-worn way off the highway. It wound into a deep cutting, and golden grasses waved above their heads at either side. Then the way rose, or the sides fell away, and the stranger looked around him at pastureland with sheep and cows grazing earnestly and solemnly across it, and then at empty meadows; and then there was a small stand of birch and ash and willow, and a small thatched house with a strictly tended herb garden around it, laid out in a maze of squares and circles and borders and low hedges. Lily swung off her small gelding at the edge of the garden and whistled: a high thin cry that told Jolin she had brought a visitor.

Jolin emerged from the house smiling. Her hair, mostly grey now, with lights of chestnut brown, was in a braid; and tucked into the first twist of the hair at the nape of her neck was a spray of yellow and white flowers. They were almost a halo, nearly a collar.

"Lady," said the stranger, and dismounted.

This is Jolin, Lily said to him. *And you*—she stopped, confused, shy again.

"Jolin," said the stranger, but Jolin did not think it odd that he knew her name, for often the villagers sent visitors on with Lily when they saw her riding by, having supplied both their names first. "I am called Sahath."

Lily moved restlessly; there was no birdcall available to her for this eventuality. She began the one for *talk*, and broke off. Jolin glanced at her, aware that something was troubling her.

Sahath, said Lily, *tell Jolin*—and her thought paused, because she could not decide, even to herself, what the proper words for it were.

But Jolin was looking at their guest more closely, and a tiny frown appeared between her eyes.

Sahath said silently to Lily, *She guesses*.

Lily looked up at him; standing side by side, he was nearly a head taller than she. *She*—?

Jolin had spent several years traveling in her youth, travelling far from her native village and even far from her own country; and on her travels she had learned more of the world than most of the other inhabitants of Rhungill, for they were born and bred to live their lives on their small land-plots, and any sign of wanderlust was firmly suppressed. Jolin, as a healer and so a little unusual, was permitted wider leeway than any of the rest of Rhungill's daughters; but her worldly knowledge was something she rarely admitted and still more rarely demonstrated. But one of the things she had learned as she and her mother drifted from town to town, dosing children and heifers, binding the broken limbs of men and pet cats, was to read the mage-mark.

"Sir," she said now, "what is one such as you doing in our quiet and insignificant part of the world?" Her voice was polite but not cordial, for mages, while necessary for some work beyond the reach of ordinary mortals, often brought with them trouble as well; and an unbidden mage was almost certainly trouble. This too she had learned when she was young.

Sahath smiled sadly. "I carry the mark, lady, it is true, but no mage am I." Jolin, staring at him, holding her worldly knowledge just behind her eyes where everything he said must be reflected through it, read truth in his eyes. "I was one once, but no longer."

Jolin relaxed, and if she need not fear this man she could pity him, for to have once been a mage and to have lost that more than mortal strength must be as heavy a blow as any man might receive and yet live; and she saw the lines of sorrow in his face.

Lily stood staring at the man with the sad face, for she knew no more of mages than a child knows of fairy tales; she would as easily have believed in the existence of tigers or of dragons, of chimeras or of elephants; and yet Jolin's face and voice were serious. A mage. This man was a mage—or had been one—and he could speak to her. It was more wonderful than elephants.

Sahath said, "Some broken pieces of my mage-truth remain to me, and one of these Lily wishes me to tell you: that I can speak to her—mind to mind."

Lily nodded eagerly, and seized her old friend and mentor's hands in hers. She smiled, pulled her lips together to whistle, "It is true," and her lips drew back immediately again to the smile. Jolin tried to smile back into the bright young face before her; there was a glow there which had never been there before, and Jolin's loving heart turned with jealousy and—fear reawakened. For this man, with his unreasonable skills, even if he were no proper mage, might be anyone in his own heart. Jolin loved Lily as much as any person may love another. What, she asked herself in fear, might this man do to her, in her innocence, her pleasure in the opening of a door so long closed to her, and open now only to this stranger? Mages were not to be trusted on a human scale of right and wrong, reason and unreason. Mages were sworn to other things. Jolin understood that they were sworn to—goodness, to rightness; but often that goodness was of a high, far sort that looked very much like misery to the smaller folk who had to live near it.

As she thought these things, and held her dearer-than-daughter's hands in hers, she looked again at Sahath. "What do you read in my mind, mage?" she said, and her voice was harsher than she meant to permit it, for Lily's sake.

Sahath dropped his eyes to his own hands; he spread the long fingers as if remembering what once they had been capable of. "Distrust and fear," he said after a moment; and Jolin was the more alarmed that she had had no sense of his scrutiny. No mage-skill she had, but as a healer she heard and felt much that common folk had no ken of.

Lily's eyes widened, and she clutched Jolin's hands. Sa-

13

hath felt her mind buck and shudder like a frightened horse, for the old loyalty was very strong. It was terrible to her that she might have to give up this wonderful, impossible thing even sooner than the brief span of an overnight guest's visit that she had promised herself—or at least freely hoped for. Even his mage's wisdom was awed by her strength of will, and the strength of her love for the aging, steady-eyed woman who watched him. He felt the girl withdrawing from him, and he did not follow her, though he might have; but he did not want to know what she was thinking. He stood where he was, the two women only a step or two distant from him; and he felt alone, as alone as he had felt once before, on a mountain, looking at a dying army, knowing his mage-strength was dying with them.

"I—" he said, groping, and the same part of his mind that had protested his halting so long before sundown protested again, saying, Why do you defend yourself to an old village woman who shambles among her shrubs and bitter herbs, mouthing superstitions? But the part of his mind that had been moved by Lily's strength and humility answered: because she is right to question me.

"I am no threat to you in any way I control," he said to Jolin's steady gaze, and she thought: Still he talks like a mage, with the mage-logic, to specify that which he controls. Yet perhaps it is not so bad a thing, some other part of her mind said calmly, that any human being, even a mage, should know how little he may control.

"It—it is through no dishonor that I lost the—the rest of my mage-strength." The last words were pulled out of him, like the last secret drops of the heart's blood of a dragon, and Jolin heard the pain and pride in his voice, and saw the blankness in his eyes; yet she did not know that he was standing again on a mountain, feeling all that had meant anything to him draining away from him into the earth, drawn by the ebbing life-force of the army he had opposed. One of the man's long-fingered hands had stretched toward the two women as he spoke; but as he said "mage-strength," the hand went to his forehead. When it dropped to his side again, there were white marks that stood a moment against the skin, where the fingertips had pressed too hard.

Jolin put one arm around Lily's shoulders and reached her other hand out delicately, to touch Sahath's sleeve. He looked up again at the touch of her fingers. "You are welcome to stay with us, Sahath."

Lily after all spoke to him very little that evening, as if, he thought, she did not trust herself, although she listened eagerly to the harmless stories he told them of other lands and peoples he had visited; and she not infrequently interrupted him to ask for unimportant details. He was careful to answer everything she asked as precisely as he could; once or twice she laughed at his replies, although there was nothing overtly amusing about them.

In the morning when he awoke, only a little past dawn, Lily was already gone. Jolin gave him breakfast and said without looking at him, "Lily has gone gathering wild herbs; dawn is best for some of those she seeks." Sahath saw in her mind that Lily had gone by her own decision; Jolin had not sent her, or tried to suggest the errand to her.

He felt strangely bereft, and he sat, crumbling a piece of sweet brown bread with his fingers and staring into his cup of herb tea. He recognized the infusion: chintanth for calm, monar for clear-mindedness. He drank what was in the cup and poured himself more. Jolin moved around the kitchen, putting plates and cups back into the cupboard.

He said abruptly, "Is there any work a simple man's strength might do for you?"

There was a rush of things through Jolin's mind: her and Lily's self-sufficiency, and their pleasure in it; another surge of mistrust for mage-cunning—suddenly and ashamedly put down; this surprised him, as he stared into his honey-clouded tea, and it gave him hope. Hope? he thought. He had not known hope since he lost his mage-strength; he had nearly forgotten its name. Jolin stood gazing into the depths of the cupboard, tracing the painted borders of vines and leaves and flowers with her eye; and now her thoughts were of things that it would be good to have done, that she and Lily always meant to see to, and never quite had time for.

When Lily came home in the late morning, a basket over her arm, Sahath was working his slow way with a spade down the square of field that Jolin had long had in her mind as an extension of her herb garden. Lily halted at the edge of the freshly turned earth, and breathed deep of the damp sweet smell of it. Sahath stopped to lean on his spade, and wiped his forehead on one long dark sleeve. *It is near dinnertime*, said Lily hesitantly, fearful of asking him why he was digging Jolin's garden; but her heart was beating faster than her swift walking could explain.

He ate with them, a silent meal, for none of the three wished to acknowledge or discuss the new balance that was already growing among them. Then he went back to his spade.

He did a careful, thorough job of the new garden plot; two

16

days it took him. When he finished it, he widened the kitchen garden. Then he built a large new paddock for Lily's horse—and his own; the two horses had made friends at once, and stood head to tail in the shade at the edge of the tiny turn-out that flanked the small barn. When they were first introduced to their new field, they ran like furies around it, squealing and plunging at each other. Jolin came out of the house to see what the uproar was about. Sahath and Lily were leaning side by side on the top rail of the sturdy new fence; Jolin wondered what they might be saying to each other. The horses had enough of being mad things, and ambled quietly over to ask their riders for handouts. Jolin turned and reentered the house.

On the third day after his arrival Jolin gave Sahath a shirt and trousers, lengthened for their new owner: The shirt tail and cuffs were wide red bands sewn neatly onto the original yellow cloth; the trousers were green, and each leg bore a new darker green hem. No mage had ever worn such garb. He put them on. At the end of the week Lily gave him a black and green—the same coarse green of the trouser-hems—jacket. He said, *Thank you, lady,* and she blushed and turned away. Jolin watched them, and wondered if she had done the right thing, not to send him away when she might have; wondered if he knew that Lily was in love with him. She wondered if a mage might know anything of love, anything of a woman's love for a man.

He propped up the sagging cow shed where the two goats lived, and made the chicken-coop decently foxproof. He built bird-houses and feeders for the many birds that were Lily's friends; and he watched her when he thought she did not notice, when they came to visit, perching on her hands and shoulders and rubbing their small heads against her face. He listened to their conversations, and knew no more of what passed than Jolin did of his and Lily's.

He had never been a carpenter, any more than he had been a gardener; but he knew his work was good, and he did not care where the skill came from. He knew he could look at the things he wished to do here and understand how best to do them, and that was enough. He slept the nights through peacefully and dreamlessly.

A few days after the gift of the jacket Jolin said to him, "The leather-worker of our village is a good man and clever. He owes us for his wife's illness last winter; it would please . . . us . . . if you would let him make you a pair of boots." His old boots, accustomed to nothing more arduous than the chafing of stirrup and stirrup-leather, had never, even in their young days, been intended for the sort of work he was lately requiring of them. He looked at them ruefully, stretched out toward the fire's flickering light, the dark green cuffs winking above them, and Karla's long furry red tail curling and uncurling above the cuffs.

He went into the village the next day. He understood, from the careful but polite greetings he received, that the knowledge of Jolin's new hired man had gone before him; and he also understood that no more than his skill with spade and hammer had gone into the tale. There was no one he met who had the skill to recognize a mage-mark, nor was there any suspicion, besides the wary observation of a stranger expected to prove himself one way or another, that he was anything more or less than an itinerant laborer. The boot-maker quietly took his measurements and asked him to return in a week.

Another week, he thought, and was both glad and afraid.

It was during that week that he finished the paddock for the horses. He wanted to build a larger shed to store hay, for there was hay enough in the meadowland around Jolin's house to keep all the livestock—even a second horse, he thought distantly—all the winter, if there was more room for it than the low loft over the small barn.

In a week he went back to fetch his boots; they were heavy, hard things, a farmer's boots, and for a moment they appalled him, till he saw the beauty of them. He thanked their maker gravely, and did not know the man was surprised by his tone. Farmers, hired men, took their footgear for granted; he had long since learned to be proud of his craft for its own sake. And so he was the first of the villagers to wonder if perhaps there was more to Jolin's hired man—other than the fact, well mulled over all through Rhungill, that Jolin had never before in over twenty years been moved to hire anyone for more than a day's specific job—than met the eye. But he had no guess of the truth.

Sahath asked the boot-maker if there was someone who sold dry planking, for he had all but used Lily and Jolin's small store of it, till now used only for patching up after storms and hard winter weather. There were several such men, and because the leather-worker was pleased at the compliment Sahath paid him, he recommended one man over the others. Sahath, unknowing, went to that man, who had much fine wood of just the sort Sahath wanted; but when he asked a price, the man looked at him a long moment and said, "No charge, as you do good work for them; you may have as much as you need as you go on for them. There are those of us know what we owe them." The man's name was Armar.

Sahath went in his heavy boots to the house he had begun

in secret to call home. He let no hint of the cost to his pride his workman's hire of sturdy boots had commanded; but still Jolin's quick eyes caught him staring at the calluses on his long-fingered hands, and guessed something of what he was thinking.

A week after he brought his boots home he began the hay shed. He also began to teach Lily and Jolin their letters. He had pen and paper in his saddlebags, and a wax tablet that had once been important in a mage's work. When he first took it out of its satchel, he had stood long with it in his hands; but it was silent, inert, a tool like a hammer was a tool and nothing more. He brought it downstairs, and whittled three styluses from bits of firewood.

"If you learn to write," he said, humbly, to Jolin, "Lily may speak to you as well as she may speak to any wandering . . . mage." It was all the explanation he gave, laying the pale smooth tablet down on the shining golden wood of the table; and Jolin realized, when he smiled uncertainly at her and then turned to look wistfully at Lily, that he did love her dearer-than-daughter, but that nothing of that love had passed between them. Jolin had grown fond of the quiet, weary man who was proving such a good landsman, fond enough of him that it no longer hurt her to see him wearing her husband's old clothes which she herself had patched for his longer frame; and so she thought, Why does he not tell her? She looked at them as they looked at each other, and knew why, for the hopelessness was as bright in their eyes as the love. Jolin looked away unhappily, for she understood too that there was no advice she could give them that they would listen to. But she could whisper charms that they permit themselves to see what was, and not blind themselves with blame for what they lacked. Her lips moved.

Each evening after that the two women sat on either side of him and did their lessons as carefully as the students of his mage-master had ever done theirs, although they had been learning words to crack the world and set fire to the seas. Sahath copied the letters of the alphabet out plainly and boldly onto a piece of stiff parchment, and Jolin pinned it to the front of the cupboard, where his two students might look at it often during the day.

Spring turned to summer, and Sahath's boots were no longer new, and he had three more shirts and another pair of trousers. The last shirt and trousers were made for him, not merely made over; and the first shirt had to be patched at the elbows. The goats produced two pair of kids, which would be sold at the fall auction in Teskip. Summer began to wane, and Sahath began to wander around the house at twilight, after work and before supper, staring at the bottles of herbs, the basket of scraps from which Jolin made her sachets, and outside in the garden, staring at the fading sun and the lengthening shadows.

Jolin thought, with a new fear at her heart, He will be leaving us soon. What of Lily? And even without thought of Lily she felt sorrow.

Lily too watched him pacing, but she said nothing at all; and what her thoughts were neither Jolin nor Sahath wished to guess.

One evening when Lily was gone to attend a sick baby, Sahath said, with the uneasy abruptness Jolin had not heard since he had asked one morning months ago if there was any work for a simple man's strength: "It is possible that I know someone who could give Lily her voice. Would you let her travel away with me, on my word that I would protect her dearer than my own life?"

Jolin shivered, and laid her sewing down in her lap. "What is this you speak of?"

Sahath was silent a moment, stroking grey tabby Annabelle. "My old master. I have not seen him since I first began . . . my travels; even now I dread going back . . . ." So much he could say after several months of farmer's labor and the companionship of two women. "He is a mage almost beyond the knowing of the rest of us, even his best pupils." He swallowed, for he had been one of these. "But he knows many things. I—I know Lily, I think, well enough to guess that her voice is something my master should be able to give her."

Jolin stared unblinking into the fire till the heat of it drew tears. "It is not my decision. We will put it to Lily. If she wishes to go with you, then she shall go."

Lily did not return till the next morning, and she found her two best friends as tired and sleepless-looking as she felt herself, and she looked at them with surprise. "Sahath said something last night that you need to hear," said Jolin; but Sahath did not raise his heavy eyes from his tea-cup.

"His . . . mage-master . . . may be able to give you your voice. Will you go with him, to seek this wizard?"

Lily's hands were shaking as she set her basket on the table. She pursed her lips, but no sound emerged. She licked her lips nervously and whistled: "I will go."

They set out two days later. It was a quiet two days; Lily did not even answer the birds when they spoke to her. They left when dawn was still grey over the trees. Jolin and Lily embraced for a long time before the older woman put the younger one away from her and said, "You go on now. Just don't forget to come back."

Lily nodded, then shook her head, then nodded again and smiled tremulously.

"I'll tell your parents you've gone away for a bit, never fear."

Lily nodded once more, slowly, then turned away to mount her little bay horse. Sahath was astride already, standing a little away from the two women, staring at the yellow fingers of light pushing the grey away; he looked down startled when Jolin touched his knee. She swallowed, tried to speak, but no words came, and her fingers dug into his leg. He covered her hand with his and squeezed; when she looked up at him, he smiled, and finally she smiled back, then turned away and left them. Lily watched the house door close behind her dearest friend, and sat immobile, staring at the place where Jolin had disappeared, till Sahath sent his horse forward. Lily awoke from her reverie, and sent the little bay after the tall black horse. Sahath heard the gentle hoofbeats behind him, and turned to smile encouragement; and Lily, looking into his face, realized that he had not been sure, even until this moment, if she would follow him or not. She smiled in return, a smile of reassurance. Words, loose and filmy as smoke, drifted into Sahath's mind: *I keep my promises*. But he did not know what she had read in his face, and he shook his head to clear it of the words that were not meant for him.

No villager would have mistaken Sahath for a workman now, in the dark tunic and cloak he had worn when he first met Lily, riding his tall black horse; the horse alone was too fine a creature for anyone but a man of rank. For all its obvious age, for the bones of its face showed starkly through the skin, it held its crest and tail high, and set its feet down as softly as if its master were made of eggshells. Lily, looking at the man beside her on his fine horse, and looking back to the pricked ears of her sturdy, reliable mount, was almost afraid of her companion, as she had been afraid when he first spoke in her mind, and as she had not been afraid again for many weeks.

Please, Sahath said now. *Do not fear me: I am the man who hammered his fingers till they were blue and black, and cursed himself for clumsiness till the birds fled the noise, and stuck his spade into his own foot and yelped with pain. You know me too well to fear me.*

Lily laughed, and the silent chime of her laughter rang in his mind as she tipped her chin back and grinned at the sky. *And I am the girl who cannot spell.*

You do very well.

Not half so well as Jolin.

Jolin is special.

Yes. And their minds fell away from each other, and each disappeared into private thoughts.

They rode south and west. Occasionally they stopped in a town for supplies; but they slept always under the stars, for Lily's dread of strangers and Sahath's uneasiness that any suspicion rest on her for travelling thus alone with him, and he a man past his prime and she a beauty. Their pace was set by Lily's horse, which was willing enough, but unaccustomed to long days of travelling, though it was young and Sahath's horse was old. But it quickly grew hard, and when they reached the great western mountains, both horses strode up the slopes without trouble.

It grew cold near the peaks, but Sahath had bought them fur cloaks at the last town; no one lived in the mountains. Lily looked at hers uncertainly, and wished to ask how it was Sahath always had money for what he wished to buy. But she did not quite ask, and while he heard the question any-way, he chose not to answer.

They wandered among the mountain crests, and Lily be-came totally confused, for sometimes they rode west and south and sometimes east and north; and then there was a day of fog, and the earth seemed to spin around her, and even her stolid practical horse had trouble finding its footing. Sahath said, *There is only a little more of this until we are clear*, and Lily thought he meant something more than the words simply said; but again she did not ask. They dismounted and led the horses, and Lily timidly reached for a fold of Sahath's sleeve, for the way was wide enough that they might walk abreast. When he felt her fingers, he seized her hand in his, and briefly he raised it to his lips and kissed it, and then they walked on hand in hand.

That night there was no sunset, but when they woke in the morning the sky was blue and cloudless, and they lay in a hollow at the edge of a sandy shore that led to a vast lake; and the mountains were behind them.

They followed the shore around the lake, and Lily whistled to the birds she saw, and a few of them dropped out of the sky to sit on Lily's head and shoulders and chirp at her.

What do the birds say to you? said Sahath, a little jealously.

Oh—small things, replied Lily, at a loss; she had never tried to translate one friend for another before. *It is not easy to say. They say this is a good place, but*—she groped for a way to explain—*different*.

Sahath smiled. *I am glad of the good, and I know of the different, for we are almost to the place we seek.*

They turned away from the lake at last, onto a narrow track; but they had not gone far when a meadow opened before them. There were cows and horses in the meadow;

they raised their heads to eye the strangers as they passed. Lily noticed there was no fence to enclose the beasts, although there was an open stable at the far edge of the field; this they rode past. A little way farther and they came to an immense stone hall with great trees closed around it, except for a beaten space at its front doors. This space was set around with pillars, unlit torches bound to their tops. A man sat alone on one of the stone steps leading to the hall doors; he was staring idly into nothing, but Lily was certain that he knew of their approach—and had known since long before he had seen or heard them—and was awaiting their arrival.

Greetings, said Sahath, as his horse's feet touched the bare ground.

The man brought his eyes down from the motes of air he had been watching and looked at Sahath and smiled. *Greetings*, he replied, and his mindspeech sounded in Lily's head as well as Sahath's. Lily clung to Sahath's shadow and said nothing, for the man's one-word *greetings* had echoed into immeasurable distances, and she was dizzy with them.

This is my master, Sahath said awkwardly, and Lily ducked her head once and glanced at the man. He caught her reluctant eye and smiled, and Lily freed her mind enough to respond: *Greetings*.

That's better, said the man. His eyes were blue, and his hair was blond and curly; if it were not for the aura of power about him that hung shivering like a cloak from his head and shoulders, he would have been an unlikely figure for a magemaster.

What did you expect, came his thought, amused, *an ancient with a snowy beard and piercing eyes—in a flowing black shroud and pointed cap?*

Lily smiled in spite of herself. *Something like that.*

The man laughed; it was the first vocal sound any of the three had yet made. He stood up. He was tall and narrow, and he wore a short blue tunic over snug brown trousers and tall boots. Sahath had dismounted, and Lily looked at the two of them standing side by side. For all the grey in Sahath's hair, and the heavy lines in his face, she could see the other man was much the elder. Sahath was several inches shorter than his master, and he looked worn and ragged from travel, and Lily's heart went out in a rush to him. The blond man turned to her at once: *You do not have to defend him from me;* and Sahath looked between them, puzzled. And Lily, looking into their faces, recognized at last the mage-mark, and knew that she would know it again if she ever saw it in another face. And she was surprised that she had not recognized it as such long since in Sahath's face, and she wondered why; and the blond man flicked another glance at her, and with the glance came a little gust of amusement, but she could not hear any words in it.

After a pause Sahath said, *You will know why we have come.*

I know. Come; you can turn your horses out with the others; they will not stray. Then we will talk.

The hall was empty but for a few heavy wooden chairs and a tall narrow table at the far end, set around a fireplace. Lily looked around her, tipping her head back till her neck creaked in protest, lagging behind the two men as they went purposefully toward the chairs. She stepped as softly as she might, and her soft-soled boots made no more noise than a cat's paws; yet as she approached the center of the great hall she stopped and shivered, for the silence pressed in on her as if it were a guardian. *What are you doing here? Why have you come to this place*? She wrapped her arms around her body, and the silence seized her the more strongly: *How dare you walk the hall of the mage-master*?

Her head hurt; she turned blindly back toward the open door and daylight, and the blue sky. Almost sobbing, she said to the silence: *I came for vanity, for vanity, I should not be here, I have no right to walk in the hall of the mage-master.*

But as she stretched out her hands toward the high doors, a bird flew through them: a little brown bird that flew in swoops, his wings closing briefly against his sides after every beat; and he perched on one of her outflung hands. He opened his beak, and three notes fell out; and the guardian silence withdrew slightly, and Lily could breathe again. He jumped from Lily's one hand to the other, and she, awed, cupped her hands around him. He cocked his head and stared at her with one onyx-chip eye and then the other. The top of his head was rust-colored, and there were short streaks of cinnamon at the corner of each black eye. He offered her the same three notes, and this time she pursed her lips and gently gave them back to him. She had bent her body over her cupped hands, and now she straightened up and, after a pause of one breath, threw her head back, almost as if she expected it to strike against something; but whatever had been there had fled entirely. The bird hopped up her wrist to her arm, to her shoulder; and then he flew up, straight up, without swooping, till he perched on the sill of one of the high windows, and he tossed his three notes back down to her again. Then two more small brown birds flew through the doors, and passed Lily so closely that her hair stirred with the wind of their tiny wings; and they joined their fellow on the windowsill. There were five birds after them, and eight after that; till the narrow sills of the tall windows were full of them and of their quick sharp song. And Lily turned away from the day-filled doorway, back to the dark chairs at the farther end of the hall, where the men awaited her.

The blond man looked long at her as she came up to him, but it was not an unkind look. She smiled timidly at him, and he put out a hand and touched her black hair. *There have been those who were invited into my hall who could not pass the door.*

Sahath's face was pale. *I did not know that I brought her—*

Into danger? finished the mage-master. *Then you have forgotten much that you should have remembered.*

Sahath's face had been pale, but at the master's words it went white, corpse-white, haggard with memory. *I have forgotten everything.*

The mage-master made a restless gesture. *That is not true; it has never been true; and if you wish to indulge in self-pity, you must do it somewhere other than here.*

Sahath turned away from the other two, slowly, as if he were an old, old man; and if Lily had had any voice, she would have cried out. But when she stepped forward to go to him, the master's hand fell on her shoulder, and she stopped where she stood, although she ached with stillness.

Sahath, the master went on more gently, *you were among the finest of any of my pupils. There was a light about you that few of the others could even see from their dulness, though those I chose to teach were the very best. Among them you shone like a star.*

Lily, the master's hand still on her shoulder, began to see as he spoke a brightness form about Sahath's hands, a shiningness, an almost-mist about his feet, that crept up his legs, as if the master's words lay around him, built themselves into a wall or a ladder to reach him, for the master's wisdom to climb, and to creep into his ear.

Sahath flung out a hand, and brightness flickered and flaked away from it, and a mote or two drifted to Lily's feet. She stooped, and touched the tips of two fingers to them, the mage-master's hand dropping away from her shoulder as she knelt. She raised her hand, and the tips of her first and third fingers glimmered.

I was the best of your pupils once, Sahath said bitterly, and the bitterness rasped at the minds that heard him. *But I did not learn what I needed most to learn: my own limits. And I betrayed myself, and your teaching, my master, and I have wandered many years since then, doing little, for little there is that I am able to do. With my mage-strength gone, my learning is of no use, for all that I know is the use of mage-strength.* He spread his hands, straightening the fingers violently as though he hated them; and then he made them into fists and shook them as if he held his enemy's life within them.

And more flakes of light fell from him and scattered, and Lily crept, on hands and knees, nearer him, and picked them up on the tips of her fingers, till all ten fingers glowed; and the knees of her riding dress shone, and when she noticed this, she laid her hands flat on the stone floor, till the palms and the finger-joints gleamed. As she huddled, bent down, her coil of hair escaped its last pins and the long braid of it fell down, and its tip skittered against the stones, and when she raised her head again, the black braid-tip was star-flecked.

The mage-master's eyes were on the girl as he said, *You betrayed nothing, but your own sorrow robbed you by the terrible choice you had to make, standing alone on that mountain. You were too young to have had to make that choice; I would have been there had I known; but I was too far away, and I saw what would happen too late. You saw what had to be done, and you had the strength to do it—that was your curse. And when you had done it, you left your mage-strength where you stood, for the choice had been too hard a one, and you were sickened with it. And you left, and I—I could not find you, for long and long. . . .* There was a weight of sorrow as bitter as Sahath's in his thought, and Lily sat where she was, cupping her shining hands in her lap and looking up at him, while his eyes still watched her. She thought, but it was a very small thought: *The silence was right—I should not be here.*

It was a thought not meant to be overheard, but the blond man's brows snapped together and he shook his head once, fiercely; and she dropped her eyes to her starry palms, and yet she was comforted.

I did not leave my mage-strength, said Sahath, still facing away from his master, and the girl sitting at his feet; but as his arms dropped to his sides, the star-flakes fell down her back and across her spreading skirts.

I am your master still, the blond man said, and his thought was mild and gentle again. *And I say to you that you turned your back on it and me and left us. Think you that you could elude me—me?—for so long had you not the wisdom I taught you—and the strength to make yourself invisible to my far-seeing? I have not known what came to you since you left that mountain with the armies dying at its feet, till you spoke of me to two women in a small bright kitchen far from here. In those long years I have known nothing of you but that you lived, for your death you could not have prevented me from seeing.*

In the silence nothing moved but the tiny wings of birds. Sahath turned slowly around.

Think you so little of the art of carpentry that you believe any man who holds a hammer in his hand for the first time may build a shed that does not fall down, however earnest his intentions—and however often he bangs his thumb and curses?

Lily saw Sahath's feet moving toward her from the corner of her eye, and lifted her face to look at him, and he looked down at her, dazed. *Lily*—he said, and stooped, but the mage-master was there before him, and took Lily's hands, and drew her to her feet. Sahath touched the star-flakes on her shoulders, and then looked at his hands, and the floor around them where the star-flakes lay like fine sand. "I—" he said, and his voice broke.

The mage-master held Lily's hands still, and now he drew them up and placed them, star-palms in, against her own throat; and curled her fingers around her neck, and held them there with his own long-fingered hands. She stared up at him, and his eyes reminded her of the doors of his hall, filled with daylight; and she felt her own pulse beating in her throat against her hands. Then the master drew his hands and hers away, and she saw that the star-glitter was gone from her palms. He dropped her hands, smiling faintly, and stepped back.

The air whistled strangely as she sucked it into her lungs and blew it out again. She opened her mouth and closed it; raised one hand to touch her neck with her fingers, yet she could find nothing wrong. She swallowed, and it made her throat tickle; and then she coughed. As she coughed, she looked down at the dark hem of her riding dress; the star-flakes were gone from it too, and the dust of them had blown away or sunk into the floor. She coughed again, and the force of it shook her whole body, and hurt her throat and lungs; but then she opened her mouth again when the spasm was past and said, "Sahath." It was more a croak, or a bird's chirp, than a word; but she looked up, and turned toward him, and said "Sahath" again, and it was a word this time. But as her eyes found him, she saw the tears running down his face.

He came to her, and she raised her arms to him; and the mage-master turned his back on them and busied himself at the small high table before the empty hearth. Lily heard the chink of cups as she stood encircled by Sahath's arms, her dark head on his dark-cloaked shoulder, and the taste of his tears on her lips. She turned at the sound, and looked over her shoulder; the master held a steaming kettle in his hands, and she could smell the heat of it, although the hearth was as black as before. Sahath looked up at his old teacher when Lily stirred; and the mage-master turned toward them again, a cup in each hand. Sahath laughed.

The mage-master grinned and inclined his head. "School-boy stuff, I know," but he held the cups out toward them nonetheless. Lily reached out her left hand and Sahath his right, so that their other two hands might remain clasped together.

Whatever the steaming stuff was, it cleared their heads and smoothed their faces, and Lily said, "Thank you," and smiled joyfully. Sahath looked at her and said nothing, and the blond man looked at them both, and then down into his cup.

"You know this place," the mage-master said presently, raising his eyes again to Sahath's shining face; "You are as free in it now as you were years ago, when you lived here as my pupil." And he left them, setting his cup down on the small table and striding away down the hall, out into the

sunlight. His figure was silhouetted a moment, framed by
the stone doorsill; and then he was gone. The small brown
birds sang farewell.

It was three days before Lily and Sahath saw him again.
For those three days they wandered together through the
deep woods around the master's hall, feeling the kindly
shade curling around them, or lifting their faces to the sun
when they walked along the shores of the lake. Lily learned
to sing and to shout. She loved to stand at the edge of the
lake, her hands cupped around her mouth, that her words
might fly as far as they could across the listening water, but
though she waited till the last far whisper had gone, she
never had an answer. Sahath also taught her to skip small
flat stones across the silver surface; she had never seen water
wider than a river before, and the rivers of her acquaintance
moved on about their business much too swiftly for any such
game. She became a champion rock-skipper; anything less
than eight skittering steps across the water before the small
missile sank, and she would shout and stamp with annoy-
ance, and Sahath would laugh at her. His stones always fled
lightly and far across the lake.

"You're *helping* them," she accused him.

"And what if I am?" he teased her, grinning.

"It's not *fair*."

The grin faded, and he looked at her thoughtfully. He
picked up another small flat stone and balanced it in his
hand. "You want to lift it as you throw it—lift it up again
each time it strikes the water. . . ." He threw, and the rock
spun and bounded far out toward the center of the lake; they
did not see where it finally disappeared.

Sahath looked at Lily. "You try."

"I—" But whatever she thought of saying, she changed her mind, found a stone to her liking, tossed it once or twice up and down in her hand, and then flicked it out over the water. They did not notice the green-crested black bird flying low over the lake, for they were counting the stone's skips; but on the fourteenth skip the bird seized the small spinning stone in its talons, rose high above the water, and set out to cross the lake.

At last the bird's green crest disappeared, and they could not make out one black speck from the haze that seemed always to muffle the farther shore.

The nights they spent in each other's arms, sleeping in one of the long low rooms that opened off each side of the mage-master's hall, where there were beds and blankets as if he had occasion to play host to many guests. But they saw no one but themselves.

The fourth morning they awoke and smelled cooking; instead of the cold food and kindling they had found awaiting their hunger on previous days, the mage-master was there, bent over a tiny red fire glittering fiercely out of the darkness of the enormous hearth at the far end of the great hall. He was toasting three thick slices of bread on two long slender sticks. When they approached him, he gravely handed the stick with two slices on it to Lily. They had stewed fruit with their toast, and milk from one of the master's cows, with the cream floating in thick whorls on top.

"It is time to decide your future," said the mage-master, and Lily sighed.

"Is it true that Sahath might have cured me . . . himself . . . at any time . . . without our having come here at all?" Her voice was still low and husky as if with disuse, but the slightly anxious tone of the query removed any rudeness it might have otherwise held.

The blond man smiled. "Yes and no. I think I may claim some credit as an—er—catalyst."

Sahath stirred in his chair, for they were sitting around the small fire, which snapped and hissed and sent a determined thread of smoke up the vast chimney.

"Sahath always was pig-headed," the master continued. "It was something of his strength and much of his weakness."

Sahath said, "And what comes to your pig-headed student now?"

"What does he wish to come to him?" his old teacher responded, and both men's eyes turned to Lily.

"Jolin is waiting for—us," Lily said. The "us" had almost been a "me"; both men had seen it quivering on her lips, and both noticed how her voice dropped away to nothing when she said "us" instead.

The mage-master leaned forward and poked the fire thoughtfully with his toasting stick; it snarled and threw a handful of sparks at him. "There is much I could teach you," he said tentatively. Lily looked up at him, but his eyes were on the fire, which was grumbling to itself; then he looked at Sahath by her side. "No," said the master. "Not just Sahath; both of you. There is much strength in you, Lily; too much perhaps for the small frame of a baby to hold, and so your voice was left behind. You've grown into it since; I can read it in your face.

"And Sahath," he said, and raised his eyes from the sulky fire to his old pupil's face. "You have lost nothing but pride and sorrow—and perhaps a little of the obstinacy. I—there is much use for one such as you. There is much use for the two of you." He looked at them both, and Lily saw the blue eyes again full of daylight, and when they were turned full on her, she blinked.

"I told Jolin I would not forget to come back," she said, and her voice was barely above a whisper. "I am a healer; there is much use for me at my home."

"I am a healer too," said the mage-master, and his eyes held her, till she broke from him by standing up and running from the hall; her feet made no more noise than a bird's.

Sahath said, "I have become a farmer and a carpenter, and it suits me; I am become a lover, and would have a wife. I have no home but hers, but I have taken hers and want no other. Jolin waits for us, for both of us, and I would we return to her together." Sahath stood up slowly; the master sat, the stick still in his hands, and watched him till he turned away and slowly followed Lily.

I hold no one against his will, the master said to his retreating back; *but your lover does not know what she is refusing, and you do know. You might—some day—tell her why it is possible to make rocks fly.*

On the next morning Lily and Sahath departed from the stone hall and the mist-obscured lake. The mage-master saw them off. He and Sahath embraced, and Lily thought, watching, that Sahath looked younger and the master older than either had five days before. The master turned to her, and held out his hands, but uncertainly. She thought he expected her not to touch them, and she stepped forward and seized them strongly, and he smiled down at her, the morning sun blazing in his yellow hair. "I would like to meet your Jolin," he said; and Lily said impulsively, "Then you must visit us."

The master blinked; his eyes were as dark as evening, and

Lily realized that she had surprised him. "Thank you," he said.

"You will be welcome in our home," she replied; and the daylight seeped slowly into his eyes again. "What is your name?" she asked, before her courage failed her.

"Luthe," he said.

Sahath had mounted already; Lily turned from the mage-master and mounted her horse, which sighed when her light weight settled in the saddle; it had had a pleasant vacation, knee-deep in sweet grass at the banks of the lake. Lily and Sahath both looked down at the man they had come so far to see; he raised a hand in farewell. Silently he said to them: *I am glad to have seen you again, Sahath, and glad to have met you, Lily.*

Lily said silently back: *We shall meet again perhaps.*

The mage-master made no immediate answer, and they turned away, and their horses walked down the path that bordered the clearing before the hill; and just as they stepped into the shade of the trees, his words took shape in their minds: *I think it very likely.* Lily, riding second, turned to look back before the trees hid him from view; his face was unreadable below the burning yellow hair.

They had an easy journey back; no rain fell upon them, and no wind chilled them, and the mountain fog seemed friendly and familiar, with nothing they need fear hidden within it; and the birds still came to Lily when she whistled to them.

They were rested and well, and anxious to be home, and they travelled quickly. It was less than a fortnight after Lily had seen the mage-master standing before his hall to bid them farewell that they turned off the main road from the

38

village of Rhungill into a deep cutting that led into the fields above Jolin's house. As Lily's head rose above the tall golden grasses, she could see the speck of color that was Jolin's red skirt and blue apron, standing quietly on the doorstep of the house, with the white birches at one side, and her herb garden spread out at her feet.

Lily's horse, pleased to be home at last, responded eagerly to a request for speed, and Sahath's horse cantered readily at its heels. They drew up at the edge of the garden, where Jolin had run to meet them. Lily dismounted hastily and hugged her.

"You see, we remembered to come back," she said.

The Stagman

She grew up in her uncle's shadow, for her uncle was made Regent when her father was placed beside her mother in the royal tomb. Her uncle was a cold, proud man, who, because he chose to wear plain clothing and to eat simple food, claimed that he was not interested in worldly things; but this was not so. He sought power as a thing to be desired of itself, to be gloated over, and to be held in a grasp of iron. His shadow was not a kind one to his niece.

She remembered her parents little, for she had been very young when they died. She did remember that they had been gentle with her, and had talked and laughed with her, and that the people around them had talked and laughed too; and she remembered the sudden silence when her uncle took their place. The silence of the following years was broken but rarely. Her maids and ladies spoke to her in whispers, and she saw no one else but her uncle, who gave her her lessons; his voice was low and harsh, and he spoke as if he begrudged her every word.

She grew up in a daze. Her lessons were always too difficult for her quite to comprehend, and she assumed that she was stupid, and did not see the glitter of pleasure in her uncle's eye as she stumbled and misunderstood. She could only guess her people's attitude toward her in the attitude of the women who served her, and none ever stayed long enough for her to overcome her shyness with them; and she had never in her life dared to ask her uncle a question. But as she grew older, it crept into her dimmed consciousness that her people had no faith in what sort of queen she might make when she came to her womanhood; she could feel their distrust in the reluctant touch of her waiting women's hands. It made her unhappy, but she was not surprised.

The country did well, or well enough, under her uncle; it did not perhaps quite prosper, as it had done in her parents' day, but it held its own. Her uncle was always fair with a terrible fairness in all his dealings, and the edge of cruelty in his fairness was so exact and subtle that no one could put a name to it. He was severe with the first man who dared question the health of the princess—too severe, with the same brilliant exactitude of his cruelty. Thus the tales of the princess's unfitness grew as swiftly as weeds in spring, while he sat silent, his hands tucked into his long white sleeves, and ruled the country, and gave the vague, pale princess the lessons she could not learn.

He might have been Regent forever, and the queen banished to a bleak country house while her spinsterhood withered to an early death. But it was not enough for him; he wanted the country well and truly in his own hands, not only in the name of the princess, his niece. She might have died mysteriously, for his scholarship included knowledge of several undetectable poisons. But that was not sufficient either, for there would be those who felt pity for the young princess, and a wistfulness that had she lived she might have outgrown the shadow of her childhood and become a good queen, for her parents had been much beloved. There might even have been a few—a very few—who wondered about the manner of her death, however undetectable the poison.

He pondered long upon it, as the princess grew toward her womanhood and the season of her name day celebration approached. He spent more time in his tower study, and when he emerged, he looked grimmer even than was his wont, and muttered of portents. The people who heard him looked over their shoulders nervously, and soon everyone in the country was saying that there were more thunderstorms than usual this year. The Regent looked more haggard as the season progressed, for he was not a very good magician—he claimed that he knew no magic, and that magic was a false branch of the tree of wisdom; but the truth was that he was too proud and secret to put himself into a master mage's hands to learn the craft of it—and the thunderstorms wearied him. But his increasingly drawn and solemn appearance worked to his advantage also, for the people took it as a sign that he grew more anxious.

The princess also was anxious, for on her name day she should be declared queen. She knew she was not fit, and she watched the sky's anger and feared that it was, as her uncle declared, a portent, and that the portent warned against her becoming queen. A relief, almost, such would be, although she was enough her parents' daughter to be ashamed of the relief, as she had long been ashamed of her lack of queenly ability. She would have gone gladly to the bleak country house—a wish flickered through her mind that perhaps away from the strict, tense life of her uncle's court she might find one or two women who would stay with her longer than a few months—and left her uncle to rule.

Then the sightings began. Her uncle was sincerely shocked when the first countryman rushed into the royal hall to babble out his story—half a man, this thing was, half a beast. But no one had seen the Regent shocked before, and those who looked on believed that the tale only confirmed the worst of his fears. But the Regent knew, hidden deep inside himself, that he was a very poor magician, and the thing he truly feared was that in his rough calling-up of storm he had set something loose that he would not be able to control.

He withdrew to his high, bare room to brood. He had ordered another storm, and it had come willingly, but he was too shaken, now, to command it, and so it loitered uncertainly on the horizon and began to break up into wandering, harmless clouds. He did not know what to do. All that night the people saw the light in his room, and told each other the story the countryman had brought—that the thing had been seen more than once; that the farmers for fear of it would not go alone to their fields—and trembled. With a wildness born of panic, at dawn the Regent collected the scattered clouds and gave the land such a storm as it had never seen; and he descended to the great public hall again, pale but composed, his hands tucked into his sleeves, while the thunder crashed and the lightning ripped outside.

That day two more messengers came, despite the storm, with stories of sightings in two more villages: that the creature was not even half a beast, but a monster, and huge; that the women and children were afraid to leave their houses even in daylight. And these villages were not so distant as was the first man's.

Even the princess heard the rumors, although she was not told what precisely the sightings were of; perhaps the women did not know either. But she understood that the sightings were of some evil thing, and that her people shrank from her the more for them. She dismissed her women, trying not to notice the relief in their faces, asking only that her meals be sent up to her private room. Even her last claim upon the royal economy was poorly delegated, and occasionally she missed a meal when no one remembered to bring her her tray; but someone remembered often enough, and she needed little food.

One day the door of her room opened, and she looked around in surprise, for she had been utterly alone for so long. Her uncle stood upon the threshold and frowned, but she was accustomed to his frowns, and saw nothing unusual.

"It is your name day," he said.

She started. "I had forgotten."

"Nonetheless, there is a . . . ritual . . . that must be performed. A ritual of . . . purification, most suitable for this day that you should have come into your queenship."

She thought she understood him, and she bowed her head; but for all the years of her uncle's domination she had a brave heart still, and it shrank with sorrow. "So be it," she whispered. When she raised her head again, she saw there were people with him; and a woman she did not recognize laid a white robe at the foot of her bed, and stepped behind the Regent again at once, as though his shadow were a protection.

"Dress yourself," said her uncle, and he and his attendants left her.

Four of the royal guard escorted her punctiliously to the great hall where her uncle was; and with him waited many other people, and she shrank from their eyes and their set, grim faces. Almost she turned and ran back to her empty room; but she was her parents' daughter, and she clenched her fingers into fists beneath the too-long sleeves, and stepped forward. Her uncle spoke no word to her, but turned to the doors that led outside; and she followed after him, her eyes fixed on the back of his white gown, that she did not have to look at all the people around her. But she heard the rustle as they followed behind.

The Regent led them out of the city, and the crowd that accompanied them grew ever greater, but none spoke. The princess kept her fists clenched at first; but she had eaten so little, and been in her small room so long, that she soon grew weary, and no longer cared for the people who followed. But her pride kept her eyes on her uncle's back, and kept her feet from stumbling. On they went, and farther on, and the sun, which had been high when they set out, sank toward twilight.

The sun was no more than a red edge on a slate grey sky when they stopped at last. It was a clear night, and one or two stars were out. Her uncle turned to face his niece and the people. "Here is the place," he said. "The place shown me in my dream, as what is to be done here was shown me." He dropped his eyes to his niece and said, "Come."

The princess followed numbly. They were in the hills beyond the city, beyond the place where her parents and their parents were buried. Beyond these hills were the farmlands that were her country's major wealth, but just here they were in wild woodland. There was a small hollow in the gentle rise of the hills, and within the hollow were standing stones that led to a black hole in one hillside; and suddenly she knew where she was, and her exhaustion left her all at once, for the terror drove it out. "No," she whispered, and put her hands to her face, and bit down on the cuff of one sleeve.

Her whisper was barely audible, but her uncle wheeled around. "I beg you," she whispered through her fingers.

"I do only what is necessary—what I was ordered to do," her uncle said, loudly, that the crowd might hear; but his voice was not low and harsh, but thin and shrill.

Desperately she turned around and stared at her people. There was light yet enough to see their faces palely looking back at her. They watched, mute and grim and expressionless. She dropped her hands and turned back to follow her uncle; oblivion seized her mind. The crowd waited at the edge of the hollow; six courtiers only followed the Regent and his niece, and at the mouth of the tunnel these courtiers paused to kindle the torches they carried. Then they entered the dark hole in the hillside.

When they reached the end of the short tunnel, the princess stopped and stared dully at the chain pegged into the rock wall; the links were rusty with disuse, for her great-grandfather had ended the sacrifices which had once been a part of the twice-yearly Festival. The only sacrifices for generations had been the sheaf of corn burnt at every threshold for the winter solstice. Dully she turned her back to the low rough wall and leaned against it, and raised her arms, the huge sleeves belling out around her like wings, that her uncle might the easier fasten the chains to her wrists. How long? she wondered, and did not know. In the old days, she had read, the priests killed the victim when he, or, rarely, she, was chained, that he might not truly suffer the agonies of thirst and starvation; and then left him there for the seven days tradition said it would have taken him to die. When the waiting was done, they took the body away and buried it honorably. She thought, wearily, that she doubted her uncle would have the mercy of the old priests.

One torch they left her; one of the courtiers tipped it against the wall, where it trailed soot up to the ceiling; then the seven of them turned and left her, never looking back, as she, wide-eyed, watched them go, and listened to the echo of their footsteps fading into silence, into the grass under the sky beyond the stony cavern in the hill.

Then she broke, and screamed, again and again, till her voice tore in her throat; and she hurled herself at the ends of the chains till her wrists were cut and bleeding; but still she pulled at her fetters and sobbed, and clawed backward at the indifferent wall, and kicked it with her soft slippered feet. Then she sank to her knees—her chains were too short to permit her to sit down—and turned her cheek against the rock, and knew no more for a time.

The ache in her shoulders and wrists woke her. The torch had nearly burnt itself out, and what light there was was dim and red and full of shadows. She sighed and stood up, and leaned against the wall again. She closed her eyes. Almost she could imagine that she heard the hill's heartbeat: a soft thud, thud. Thud.

Her eyes flew open. I am no Festival offering, she thought. I've been left for the monster; the monster has come for my name day. That is why I am here. A ritual of purification— if it is my fault the thing came, then perhaps I do belong to it; gods, I can't bear it, and she bit down a scream. Thud. Thud. Please make it hurry. She gave a last horrible, hopeless jerk at her chains, but her mind was too clear for this now, and the pain stopped her at once. The torch flickered and burnt lower yet, and for a moment she did not recognize the antler shadows from the other shadows on the low smoky wall. Then she saw his great head with the wide man's shoulders beneath it, the stag pelt furring him down to his chest. But it was a man's body, naked and huge, and a man's huge hands; and panic seized her, and she screamed again, though her voice was gone and the noise was only a hoarse gasp. But the stag head's brown eyes saw the cords that stood out on her neck, and saw the terror that pressed her against the wall. He had taken soft, slow steps thus far, but now he hurried, and his huge hands reached out for her. She had just the presence of mind to be able to close her eyes, though she could not avoid the warm animal smell of him; and she felt his hands close around her bleeding wrists, and she fainted.

She came to herself lying stretched out on the ground. She was not sprawled, as though she had fallen, but rested peacefully on her back, her poor sore wrists laid across her stomach. She blinked; she had not been unconscious long, for the torch still burnt, guttering, and by its light she saw an immense shadow looming over her, that of a stag, with antlers so wide he must turn his head with care in the narrow tunnel. She raised herself to her elbows, wincing at her shoulders' protest. Surely . . . ? The stag looked gravely down at her. She sat up the rest of the way, and gingerly touched one wrist with a finger. The stag stepped forward and lowered his nose between her hands; his eyes were so dark she could not see into them, and his breath smelled of sweet grass. "Yes, they are sore," she said to him stupidly, and he raised his great head again, the heavy, graceful neck proudly balancing his crown. How did I . . . ? Did I imagine . . . ? She looked at the wall. The chains had been pulled clear out of the wall, their staples bowed into broken-backed arches; they lay on the floor near her, flakes of rust mixing with smears of fresh blood.

The stag dropped his nose again, and touched her shoulder as gently as a snowflake landing, or a mare greeting a new foal. She stood up as shakily as any foal; her head swam. Then she took an eager step forward, toward the other end of the tunnel, toward the grass and the sky—but the stag stepped before her, and blocked her way. "But . . ." she said, and her eyes filled with the tears of final exhaustion, of desolation of spirit. The stag knelt before her. At first she did not understand, and would have stepped over and around him, but he was stubborn. She seated herself meekly on his back at last, and he rose gently and walked out of the cave.

She shivered when the first breath of air from the hill touched her face, although it was a warm night. She looked up in wonder at the sky, and the stars twinkling there; she could not believe she had spent so little time in the tunnel, leaning against the rock wall, with her arms aching and her mind holding nothing but despair. She looked uncertainly back the way her uncle had led them, though she could not see far for the trees that ringed the small valley. But it seemed to her that the shadows under the trees were of more things than leaves and stones, and some of them were the shapes of human watchers; and it seemed to her too that a low murmur, as from human throats, rose and mixed with the gentle wind; but the murmur was a sound of dismay. The stag paused a moment a few steps beyond the cave's threshold, and turned his fine head toward the murmur, toward the path to the city; then he turned away and entered the forest by a path only he could see.

They stopped at dawn, and he knelt for her to dismount; she stretched her sore limbs with a sigh, and sat stiffly down.

The next thing she knew it was twilight again, the sun setting, and a small fire burnt near her, and beside that lay a heap of fruit. There were several small apples, and sweet green gurnies, which must have come from someone's orchard, for the gurny tree did not grow wild so far north. She did not care where they had come from, though, and she ate them hungrily, and the handful of kok-nuts with them. She recognized the sound of a stream nearby, and went toward it, and was glad of a drink and a wash, though she hissed with pain as she rubbed the caked scabs on her wrists. When she returned to the little fire, the great stag was standing beside it. He stamped the fire out with his forefeet and came to her and knelt, and she trustfully and almost cheerfully climbed onto his back.

They travelled thus for three nights. Each evening she awoke to a fire and to a small offering of fruit and nuts; but she had never eaten much, and it was plenty to sustain her. Even though she did not know it, her eyes grew brighter, and a little color crept back to her pale face; but only the stag saw, and he never spoke. On the third morning, though she lay down as she had done before, she did not sleep well, and once or twice she half awoke. The second time she felt a flickering light against her closed eyelids, and sleepily she opened them a little. A huge man knelt beside a small fire, setting down a small pile of fruit beside it, and then prodding it with a stick to make it burn up more brightly. He stood up beside it then and held his hands out as if to warm them. He was naked, though his heavy hair fell past his shoulders, and his thick beard mixed with the mat of hair on his chest and down his belly. His hair was a deep red brown, like the color of a deer's flank, and the bare skin beyond was much the same color. If this were not enough to know him by, the antlers that rose from his human head would have reassured her. She closed her eyes again and drifted peacefully back to sleep; and when she awoke at twilight, the stag lay curled up with his legs folded neatly under him and the tip of his nose just resting on the ground.

That night they climbed a hill face so steep that she had to cling to his antlers to prevent herself from sliding backward; the incline did not seem to distress him, although she could feel the deep heave of his breathing between her knees. About midnight they came to a level place, and she saw that a vast lake stretched to their right, and the moon shone silver upon its untroubled surface. She could not see its farther shore; the silver faded to blackness beyond the edge of her eyesight. The stag stood for a few moments till his breathing calmed, and then took a path that led them away from the lake, through more trees, and then to a broad field that smelled sweetly of grass and sleeping cattle, and then into more trees. But something now twinkled at them from beyond the trees; something too low and golden for a star. Her heart sank. She had thought as little as she might for the past four nights; she knew irresistibly that she must be being carried to somewhere, but she was sorry that the somewhere was so close. She reached out and grasped a silky-smooth horn. "Stop," she said. "Please."

He stopped and turned his head a little that he might roll one brown eye back at her. She slipped off his back and stood hesitating. Then she laid a hand on his shoulder and said, "Very well." He stepped forward, and she kept pace at his side.

The golden twinkle resolved itself into a ring of torches set on slender columns in a semicircle around a small, bare courtyard before a great stone hall. The stag walked without pause up the low steps to the door, a door high and wide enough even for his branching crown. Still she kept pace, and before her was a vast chamber, dimly lit by a fire in a hearth at its far end. There were several tall chairs before the fire, and from the shadows of one of them a tall narrow man with pale hair stood up and came toward them. "Welcome, child," he said to her; and to him, "Thank you."

She did not care for the big hall; it was too large and too empty, and the shadows fell strangely from its corners; and the last roof she had stood under had also been of stone—she shuddered. She would not pass these doors. The man saw the shudder and said gently, "It's all over now. You're quite safe." She looked up at him—he was very tall—and wanted to say, "How do you know?" But if she asked one question, a hundred would follow, and she was tired, and lonely, and had been trained never to ask questions.

She did not remember if it was the stag or the tall man who showed her to the long narrow room with the row of empty beds in it; she woke up burrowed in blankets in the bed nearest the door, with sunlight—late-morning sunlight, she estimated, blinking—flaming through the row of windows high above her head.

Her sleeping hall, she discovered, was built out from one wall of the great central chamber she had peered into the night before. The tall man sat on the front steps she had climbed, her hand on the stag's shoulder, the night before; his long hands dangled idly between his bent knees. He looked up at her as she stepped from the sleeping hall; his hair blazed as yellow as corn in the sunlight. He wore a plain brown tunic over pale leggings and soft boots, and around his neck on a thong was a red stone. She turned away from him; around her on three sides were trees, and on the fourth side, the great grey hall; overhead the sky was a clear, hard blue. She lowered her eyes, finally, and met the man's gaze; he smiled at her.

"I am Luthe," he said.

She did not answer immediately. "I am Ruen. But you know that, or I would not be here." Her voice—she could not help it—had a sharp, mistrustful edge to it.

Luthe spread his fingers and looked down at them. "That is not precisely true. I did not know your name till now, when you told it to me. Your . . . difficulties . . . were brought to my attention recently, and it is true that I asked, um, a friend if he would help you out of them. And I asked him to bring you here."

"A friend," she said, the edge to her voice gone. She closed her eyes a moment; but there was little she cared to remember, and she opened them again, and tried to smile. "It is pleasanter to thank you—and him—without thinking about what, and how much, I have to be grateful to you for." She paused. "I would like to declare, here, today, that I have no past. But then I have no future either. Have you a use for me?"

"Yes," said Luthe.

"I suppose you will now tell me that I may not forsake my past so? Well. I am not surprised. I never learned so much as . . . my uncle wished to teach me, but I did learn a little."

"You learned far more than he wished you to," Luthe said grimly. "Had you cooperated to the extent of idiocy, as would have pleased him best, he would not have had to disturb the weather for half the world to invent portents for his insignificant corner of it."

She smiled involuntarily. She had never heard anyone

speak with less than complete respect of the Regent; and these few words from this strange man reduced her uncle to nothing more than a nuisance, a bothersome thing to be dealt with; and suddenly her past was not the doom of her future. "That awful weather was *his* . . . ?" She sobered. "But I am still a poor excuse for a queen, even if he is not a—an entirely honorable Regent."

Luthe laughed. "You are wrong, my child. Only a real queen could call that poison-worm only 'not entirely honorable.' The defects in your education can be mended." He stood up, and bowed. "Which is the first item on our agenda. We will do our poor best to look after certain historical and philosophical aspects. . . ." He paused, for she was looking at him uneasily.

"Truly I am not good at lessons," she said.

"You wouldn't know," Luthe said cheerfully. "You've never had any. With me you will have real lessons. And your . . . um . . . lesson in practical application will be along presently."

"Will I—may I—see my . . . the stag again?"

"Yes," said Luthe. "He will return. Come along now."

She sighed, but the custom of obeying orders was strong.

She had no way of knowing it, but visitors to Luthe's mountain often found themselves a little vague about the passing of the days. There was something about the air that was both clearer and fuzzier than the air she was accustomed to; she slept heavily and dreamlessly and woke up feeling happy. She learned a great deal in a very short time, and was astonished to discover she could.

"Do stop giving me that fish-eyed look," Luthe said irritably; "I'm not magicking anything over on you. You have a perfectly good brain, once you are permitted to use it. Your uncle's absence provides permission. Now pay attention and don't brood."

One morning Luthe announced, "No lessons today. I anticipate visitors." She looked up in alarm. She had seen no one but Luthe since the stag had brought her here, and she knew at once that the visitors would have something to do with her future. She tried not to be dismayed, but she was still enjoying the novelty of enjoying anything, and dreaded interruption; the habit of pessimism was not easily shaken, even by Luthe's teaching.

Soon she heard the sound of . . . something . . . making its way through the trees around the courtyard where they sat. Just before she saw the great stag separate himself from the shadows of the trees Luthe stood up. The stag's footfalls were soft; the noise was made by someone who staggered along beside him, one arm over his neck. This man wore tattered leggings under a long white tunic, now torn and dirty, the left side matted brown and adhering to his side. The stag stopped just inside the ring of trees. "Oof," said the man, and fell to the ground.

"You needn't have half killed him," Luthe said. "You might also have carried him here." The stag looked at Luthe, who shrugged. "Perhaps. Perhaps not. Well, he is here, which is what matters."

Ruen stared at the stag, who turned his head to return her gaze; but if he said anything to her, she did not hear it.

"*Ruen*," Luthe said, and she realized by his tone that he had repeated her name several times.

"I ask pardon," she said, and snapped her eyes away from the stag's.

Luthe looked at her and smiled faintly. "Here is the practical lesson I promised you."

She blinked, and glanced down at the man on the ground. He stirred and moaned; the moan had words in it. She knelt beside him, and his eyes flickered open, saw her, tried to focus on her. "Ugh?" he muttered. "Uh. Oh." His eyes closed again.

"I suggest you get him to the nearest bed in the nearest sleeping hall," Luthe said briskly, "and I will join you in a little time and tell you what to do next."

The man on the ground was a lot bigger than she was, but she lifted one of his arms to drag it around her shoulders. He feebly tried to help, and she managed to get him to his feet. "Sorry," he muttered in her ear. "Not feeling quite . . . well."

They stumbled the few steps to the nearer of the two long sleeping rooms, and she hauled him up the few steps to the doorway, and tried to lower him gently onto the first bed; but his weight was too much for her, and he fell with a grunt. Luthe arrived then, and handed her warm water in a basin, and herbs and ointment, and long cloths for bandages, and a knife to cut away the stained tunic. She'd never dressed a wound before, but her hands were steady, and Luthe's patient voice told her exactly what to do, although he did not touch the man himself. The wound, or wounds, were curious; there were two neat round holes in the man's side, one of them deep and the second, a hand's length distant, little more than a nick in the skin. She stared at them as she bathed the man's side; they might have been made by a blow from a huge stag's antlers.

When she had done all she could to Luthe's satisfaction

and could at last leave the man's bedside, the stag was nowhere to be found.

She slept in the bed next to his that night, with a fat candle
burning on a little table between them, but he slept peacefully, and when she rose at dawn and blew the candle out,
she stood looking down on the man's quiet face, and noticed
that he was handsome.

Later that morning he awoke and, when he discovered her
sitting beside him, said, "I'm hungry." When she brought
him food, he had pulled himself nearly to a sitting position
against the bedhead, but his face said that it had not been a
pleasant effort; and he let her feed him without protest.

On the second day he asked her name. She was tending
his side and she said, "Ruen," without looking up.

On the third day he said, "My name's Gelther."

She smiled politely and said, "My honor is in your acquaintance."

He looked at her thoughtfully. "Where I come from we
say, 'My honor is yours.' You must be from the south. And
you must be of high blood or you wouldn't be talking of
honor at all."

"Very well. I am from the south, and I am of high blood.
Both these things I would have told you, had you asked."

He looked embarrassed. "I apologize, lady. It's a habit, I
believe. I've been told before that I'm better at doing things
than I am at making conversation. Although I'm not sure if
talking to the lady who binds your wounds and feeds you
with a spoon when you're too weak to sit up is making
conversation." She said nothing, and after a moment he went
on. "The only Ruen I know of is a princess who disappeared

mysteriously a few months ago. . . . I'm doing it again, aren't I?"

She nodded, but asked with a careful casualness, "What kind of mystery was she supposed to have disappeared in?"

She could see him considering what to tell her. "The tales vary. She was old enough to be declared queen, but she—there was something supposed to be wrong with her. This, um, ritual, might have cured it. . . ."

She laughed: the noise startled her, for she would not have thought that such a description of her uncle's perfidy would have struck her so. "I ask pardon. That ritual, had it been completed to expectation, would certainly have cured her."

Gelther eyed her. "They do say the rite went awry somehow. And we always did think there was something a little odd about the Regent."

"Yes." She frowned.

Gelther said, half-desperately, "*Are* you that Ruen?"

"Eh? Oh, yes—of course." Satisfaction and puzzlement chased each other across the young man's face. "But you heard that that Ruen had the mind of a child who could never grow up, which is why her name was not given her properly upon her name day, as a queen's should; but I seem quite normal?" Now embarrassment joined the puzzlement, and satisfaction disappeared. "I would not have grown up had I not been rescued and brought here. . . . But I almost wish I had not."

Gelther said, astonished: "Why ever not?"

She looked at his open, bewildered face. "Because I do not know what I must do. When I believed in my uncle and not in myself, I needed do nothing. I see that my uncle is not as I believed; but I am not accustomed to practical matters—to action—and I am afraid of him." She sighed. "I am terribly afraid of him."

"Well, of course you are," said Gelther stoutly. "I have heard—" He stopped, and smiled crookedly. "Never mind what I have heard. But perhaps I can help you. This is the sort of thing I'm good at—plotting and planning, you know, and then making a great deal of noise till things get done."

She looked at him wistfully and wished she could feel even a little of his enthusiasm for what such a task was likely to entail.

Gelther was walking, slowly and stiffly, but walking, in five days, and had his first independent bath in the bath-house behind the stone hall on the sixth. Luthe was never around when Gelther was awake; Gelther had asked, on that fifth day, when he went outside the sleeping room for the first time and saw nothing around him but trees, "Are you alone here?" His tone of voice suggested barely repressed horror.

"No, no, of course not," she responded soothingly. "But our host is, um, shy." She found the solitude so pleasant that she had to remind herself that not everyone might find it so.

But she did wonder at Luthe's continued elusiveness; she saw him herself every day, but always, somehow, just after Gelther had nodded into another convalescent nap. That fifth day, she taxed him with it. He replied placidly, "He's your practical lesson, not mine. We will meet eventually. Don't worry. You shan't have to explain my vagaries much longer."

She showed Gelther the way to the wide silver lake, and they walked there together. "Where is your country?" she asked, a little hesitantly, for fear that he might think she was taking a liberty.

He laughed. "I thought you were never going to ask me that," he said. "No . . . I'm not offended. I'm from Vuek, just north of your Arn—I meant only that I cannot understand how you have not asked before. I asked you at once—indirectly perhaps, but I did ask."

She nodded, smiling. "I remember. That is different, somehow. You were the one in bed, and I was the one standing on my feet. You needed to know."

He looked at her. "I always need to know."

They came to the lake, and found a log to lean against, and sat down, Gelther very carefully. Then she asked the question that she had wished and feared to ask since she first saw the wounds in his side. "How—how did you happen to come here?"

He frowned, staring off over the lake. "I'm not sure. I don't remember much of it. At home, I hunt a lot when there isn't anything else to do, and the tale was brought to me of a huge stag that had been sighted a way off, and I thought to track it. They said it had a rack of antlers the like of which had never been seen anywhere, and they knew I would be interested. I'm a good tracker, I would have found it anyway; but it was so damn easy to find you'd think it was waiting for me. . . ." His voice trailed off. "So, I found it, and it led me a fine dance, but my blood was up and I would have followed it across the world. And it turned on me. Deer don't, you know—at least not unless one is wounded to death, and cornered. And this great beast—I'd been following it for days by then, and we were both pretty weary, but I'd never gotten close enough to it even to try to put an arrow in it—and it turned on me." His voice was bewildered, and then reminiscent. "It did have antlers like nothing I've seen. It was a great chase. . . . I don't remember after that. I woke up . . . here

63

. . . and there you were, the little lost princess from Arn."
He smiled at her and it occurred to her that he was trying to
be charming, so she smiled back. "Maybe I'm supposed to
help you," he said.

It was her turn to look out over the lake. That, I suppose,
is what Luthe has had in mind all along, she thought, and
suddenly felt tired.

The next morning Luthe presented himself to Gelther for
the first time. "Prince," said Luthe, and bowed; and Gelther
glanced sidelong at Ruen to make sure she registered the title
before he bowed back. "Forgive my long delay in greeting
you."

Gelther accepted the lack of explanation with what seemed
to Ruen uncharacteristic docility, but after Luthe had left
them, he said to her accusingly, "You didn't tell me he was
a mage."

"I didn't know," said Ruen.

"Didn't . . . ? By the Just and Glorious, can't you read the
mage-mark?"

"No," she said, and he shook his head; and she thought
that for the first time he understood the boundaries of her
life with her uncle; it was as though she had said she had
never seen the sky, or never drunk water.

Luthe said, at their next meeting, "I am glad to see you
recovering so quickly from your hurt."

"I have had excellent care," said Gelther, and smiled at
Ruen, who fidgeted. "And I thank you, sir, for your hospital-
ity—"

"You are welcome to all that my house may afford you,"
Luthe interrupted smoothly. "And as soon as you are quite
healed—for you are a little weak yet, I believe—I will set you
on your way home again."

Prince Gelther, however forthright he might be to common mortals, had the sense to leave mages well enough alone, so he did not inquire how he happened to be here or where here was. Ruen could see these questions and others battering at one another behind his eyes, and she could guess that Luthe saw them too; but none escaped Gelther's lips, and Luthe offered nothing but a smile and a bright blue glint from half-shut eyes.

"Sir," said Gelther carefully. "I would ask . . . perhaps a great favor."

"Say it," said Luthe, with the careless generosity of a great lord who may instantly retract if he chooses.

"I would beg leave to take the lady Ruen with me, for I believe that I might help her, and her country and her people, escape the heavy reign of the false Regent."

"An excellent plan," said Luthe. "I applaud and bless it." Ruen sighed.

They set out a few days later, on foot, bearing a small, heavy bundle each, of food wrapped up in a thin blanket; it was nearing summer, and travel was easy. Luthe bade them farewell in the small court before his hall; he was at his most dignified with Gelther, although his words were cordial. But he set his hands on Ruen's shoulders and stared down at her with almost a frown on his face. "Gelther is a very able man," he said at last; "you and your country are fortunate to have gained him as an ally."

"Yes," Ruen said dutifully.

Luthe dropped his hands. "You were *born* to be queen," he said plaintively. "There is a limit to the miracles even I can produce."

"Yes," repeated Ruen. "I thank you for all you have done."

"Ah, hells," said Luthe.

Gelther and Ruen went down hill all that day, and the trees were so tall and thick they could not see the sun but in occasional flashes, useless to give them a sense of direction; but Luthe had told them to go down hill, and that they would not lose themselves, and Luthe was a mage, so they did as he said. They went down hill the second day as well, sliding on the steep bits and holding on to convenient branches; and in the afternoon the trees grew thin and the slope eased, and Gelther said, "I know where we are!" and strode off purposefully. Ruen followed.

She did not know what she was expecting from Vuek, or from Gelther's family; but they greeted her with pleasure—almost with relief, she thought, for Gelther was a third son, and it was obvious, although perhaps not to Gelther himself, that his father, mother, and eldest brother had begun to wonder how much longer their small kingdom could contain him. Everyone believed her story at once; or if any had doubts, they were swiftly set aside, for several aristocratic Arnish families, tiring of the Regent's inelegance, if not his tyranny, had emigrated to Vuek, and the manner in which her subjects-in-exile greeted Ruen left no room for question. There was even one woman among these who had borne brief service as the young princess's waiting maid, and if Ruen felt that the woman's eagerness to prove her loyalty now was a little overemphatic, she did not say so aloud.

Soon Gelther, and a few of the Arnish men, were out rousing the countryside; and sooner than it took Ruen to wonder what the next step should be, there was an army, forming up for drill in the fields surrounding Vuek's capital city.

A week before they were due to march to Arn, Gelther and

Ruen were married. Gelther's mother planned and arranged it; Ruen stood quietly where she was put while gowns were pinned on her and shoes cut and fitted, and hairdressers tried for the style best suited to her small solemn face. When the day came, Gelther took a few hours off from enthusiastic drilling to stand at Ruen's side while the priests muttered over them and the girls of the royal family threw flowers over them, and all the aristocracy available from Vuek and Arn and the other small kingdoms and duchies who were providing soldiers for Gelther's army made obeisances at them; and then he rushed back to his military maneuvers. Ruen retired to a handsome, well-furnished room that her new mother had set aside for her, for she was to have no part in the restoration of her throne.

Gelther was preoccupied on their wedding night, but then so was Ruen.

But Arn was taken without a sword's being drawn. Vuek had a common border with Arn, if a short one, and Gelther's soldiers marched directly to the Regent's palace; they saw few farmers in the fields, and those they saw avoided them; the streets of the city were empty, and when they reached the palace itself, the few guards they found were sitting or wandering dazedly, and when ordered to lay down their weapons, they did so without demur. Gelther and his captains strode through the front doors without any to say them nay; and when they reached the great hall where the throne stood, and where the Regent was accustomed to meet those who would speak with him, it was empty but for a few courtiers. These courtiers only turned to look at the invaders.

One shook himself free of the vagueness that held everyone else; and he came toward them, and bowed low. He wore no sword or knife. He said to Gelther, who was obviously the leader, "You will be Prince Gelther, husband of our beloved queen, whom we look forward to welcoming soon, when she returns to her land and her people. We wept when she left us, and turned our faces from the Regent, and have hoped upon each dawning that it heralded the day she would come back to us."

Gelther exchanged looks with his captains, and all grasped their sword hilts in expectation of a trap. But there was no trap.

The Regent's body they found, as the courtiers had found it two days before, bowed over a long table in the high tower room where he had called the storms and watched for portents. His lips were writhed back over his teeth in a grimace, but it appeared to be a grimace of anger; he did not look as though he had died in pain, and there was no mark on him. His captains shivered, but Gelther said, "The man is dead, and he was Regent, and my wife's uncle; and that is all we need now remember. The people have declared that they wish to welcome us; so let us allow ourselves to be welcome."

They buried the Regent with restrained pomp and the respect that might have been due a queen's uncle who had stood by her and cared for her when her parents died while she was yet too young to rule herself. Gelther, who knew much more about the Regent than he would ever have admitted to his wife, would let no man say a word against him. None ever knew if he had died naturally, or been slain, by his own hand, or another's; perhaps even by a portent he had wrongly tried to call up.

Her people did indeed honor their queen when she returned to them; they could not leap quickly enough to do her bidding, smile quickly enough when her eye fell upon them, clamor loudly enough to serve her, spread quickly enough

68

the tales of her evenhanded justice, of her kindness to the weak and patience with the confused. But their hearts were perhaps particularly captured by the prince, who was loud and strong and merry—it was noticed that the queen never laughed—and who refused to be crowned king in deference to his wife, who, he said, "is the real thing." And of course, the people of Arn had seen Gelther only in triumph, and the fact that the queen did not find anything in her native land to rouse her to laughter perhaps stirred memories they wished to forget.

Gelther also made Arn's army the finest in the whole of the Damarian continent, and all the countries near Arn were very careful to stay on the most cordial terms with it; and the Arnish families' greatest pride was to have a son or two or three in the prince's army. A goodly number of the young men who flocked to carry the Arnish prince's banner came from other countries, for tales of the prince's greatness travelled far.

Ruen bore four children, all sons; and she was kind and loving to them, and they responded with kindness and love. But, although there was perhaps no one to notice, her maternal kindness was little more exacting than the kindness she gave the least of her subjects who pleaded for her aid. But perhaps it was only that she had so little in common with her children; for while her sons treated her always with respect, they thought of nothing but the army once they were old enough to be propped up on their first ponies.

The people did notice that the queen seemed most at ease with folk young enough not to remember the days of the Regent's rule; but her people chose to tell one another that many women are happiest in the company of those they may pretend are their children, and such a one was their queen.

It had been only a very short time after Gelther accepted the Arnish welcome in the queen's name that all her subjects were eager to tell her that they had forgotten the Regent entirely—and the longer anyone had lived under him, the more eager he was to proclaim his complete lack of memory—if she had asked; but she never asked.

Her youngest son was eleven years old and would soon outgrow his third pony the morning that her eldest burst in on his parents' quiet breakfast. "Father! We go hunting today! There are sightings of a great stag—as large as the one that gored you when you met Mother—to the northwest. *Several* sightings. He's been showing himself to different villages but everyone's been afraid to mention it . . . seems they think he's half man or something, and an ill portent—some nonsense about something my stupid great-uncle did. You'd think they'd have forgotten by now."

"No." It was so unusual for the queen to say anything when the conversation turned to hunting that both Gelther and their son gaped at her.

Gelther swallowed. "No . . . er . . . what?"

"No, you will not hunt this stag. I insist." She opened her wide eyes wider and fixed them on her handsome husband. "You shall *not* go."

It was a struggle for Gelther, for he loved hunting best of anything when there were no wars to be fought; but he was fond of his wife, and she had never asked him such a thing before. Indeed, she asked him little enough at any time—and, well, she was a woman, and the Regent had been very queer to her for many years, and it was perhaps understandable that she should be a little, well, superstitious about something that reminded her so suddenly of the bad old days. She'd been the one who'd patched him up then too; it had probably been worse for her. And the villagers were probably exaggerating the beast's size anyway. "Very well," he said, a little wistfully.

She smiled at him, and there was such love in her eyes that he smiled back, thinking, I could not have had a better wife; four sons she's given me. Then he rose from the table and slapped his eldest on the shoulder and said, "So, my son, we must find our amusement elsewhere; have you tried the new colt I bought at the Ersk fair? I think he'll just suit you."

Two days later the queen walked out of the palace in the early afternoon, alone. She often did; she liked to visit the tomb of her parents on the hill beyond the city by herself; and her waiting women and royal guards, who would rather have made a parade out of it, had grown accustomed to the queen's small eccentricity, and no longer thought anything of it. But this time she did not return. A great hue and cry went up, in Arn and in Vuek and everywhere that messengers could go, from the mountains east, north, and west, even beyond the desert in the south to the great sea; but she was never seen again by anyone who brought word back to her mourning husband and country.

The villagers who had been frightened by the reappearance of the great stagman, as they had first seen him twenty years ago, were relieved when he disappeared again; and since news travelled slowly and erratically to them, none noticed that the stagman vanished for the second and final time two days after the Arnish queen walked out of her palace and did not return.

Touk's House

There was a witch who had a garden. It was a vast garden, and very beautiful; and it was all the more beautiful for being set in the heart of an immense forest, heavy with ancient trees and tangled with vines. Around the witch's garden the forest stretched far in every direction, and the ways through it were few, and no more than narrow footpaths.

In the garden were plants of all varieties; there were herbs at the witch's front door and vegetables at her rear door; a hedge, shoulder-high for a tall man, made of many different shrubs lovingly trained and trimmed together, surrounded her entire plot, and there were bright patches of flowers scattered throughout. The witch, whatever else she might be capable of, had green fingers; in her garden many rare things flourished, nor did the lowliest weed raise its head unless she gave it leave.

There was a woodcutter who came to know the witch's garden well by sight; and indeed, as it pleased his eyes, he found himself going out of his way to pass it in the morning as he began his long day with his axe over his arm, or in the evening as he made his way homeward. He had been making as many of his ways as he could pass near the garden for some months when he realized that he had worn a trail outside the witch's hedge wide enough to swing his arms freely and let his feet find their own way without fear of clutching roots or loose stones. It was the widest trail anywhere in the forest.

The woodcutter had a wife and four daughters. The children were their parents' greatest delight, and their only delight, for they were very poor. But the children were vigorous and healthy, and the elder two already helped their mother in the bread baking, by which she earned a little more money for the family, and in their small forest-shadowed village everyone bought bread from her. That bread was so good that her friends teased her, and said her husband stole herbs from the witch's garden, that she might put it in her baking. But the teasing made her unhappy, for she said such jokes would bring bad luck.

And at last bad luck befell them. The youngest daughter fell sick, and the local leech, who was doctor to so small a village because he was not a good one, could do nothing for her. The fever ate up the little girl till there was no flesh left on her small bones, and when she opened her eyes, she did not recognize the faces of her sisters and mother as they bent over her.

"Is there nothing to do?" begged the woodcutter, and the doctor shook his head. The parents bowed their heads in despair, and the mother wept.

A gleam came into the leech's eyes, and he licked his lips nervously. "There is one thing," he said, and the man and his wife snapped their heads up to stare at him. "The witch's garden . . ."

"The witch's garden," the wife whispered fearfully.

"Yes?" said the woodcutter.

"There is an herb that grows there that will break any fever," said the doctor.

"How will I know it?" said the woodcutter.

The doctor picked up a burning twig from the fireplace, stubbed out the sparks, and drew black lines on the clean-swept hearth. "It looks so—" And he drew small three-lobed leaves. "Its color is pale, like the leaves of a weeping willow, and it is a small bushy plant, rising no higher than a man's knee from the ground."

Hope and fear chased themselves over the wife's face, and she reached out to clasp her husband's hand. "How will you come by the leaves?" she said to him.

"I will steal them," the woodcutter said boldly.

The doctor stood up, and the woodcutter saw that he trembled. "If you . . . bring them home, boil two handsful in water, and give the girl as much of it as she will drink." And he left hastily.

"Husband—"

He put his other hand over hers. "I pass the garden often. It will be an easy thing. Do not be anxious."

On the next evening he waited later than his usual time for returning, that dusk might have overtaken him when he reached the witch's garden. That morning he had passed the garden as well, and dawdled by the hedge, that he might mark where the thing he sought stood; but he dared not try his thievery then, for all that he was desperately worried about his youngest daughter.

He left his axe and his yoke for bearing the cut wood leaning against a tree, and slipped through the hedge. He was surprised that it did not seem to wish to deter his passage, but yielded as any leaves and branches might. He had thought at least a witch's hedge would be full of thorns and brambles, but he was unscathed. The plant he needed was near at hand, and he was grateful that he need not walk far from the sheltering hedge. He fell to his knees to pluck two handsful of the life-giving leaves, and he nearly sobbed with relief.

"Why do you invade thus my garden, thief?" said a voice behind him, and the sob turned in his throat to a cry of terror.

He had never seen the witch. He knew of her existence because all who lived in the village knew that a witch lived in the garden that grew in the forest; and sometimes, when he passed by it, there was smoke drifting up from the chimney of the small house, and thus he knew someone lived there. He looked up, hopelessly, still on his knees, still clutching the precious leaves.

He saw a woman only a little past youth to look at her, for her hair was black and her face smooth but for lines of sorrow and solitude about the mouth. She wore a white apron over a brown skirt; her feet were bare, her sleeves rolled to the elbows, and her hands were muddy.

"I asked you, what do you do in my garden?"

He opened his mouth, but no words came out; and he shuddered till he had to lean his knuckles on the ground so that he would not topple over. She raised her arm, and pushed her damp hair away from her forehead with the back of one hand; but it seemed, as he watched her, that the hand, as it fell through the air again to lie at her side, flickered through some sign that briefly burned in the air; and he found he could talk.

"My daughter," he gasped. "My youngest daughter is ill . . . she will die. I—I stole these"—and he raised his hands pleadingly, still holding the leaves which, crushed between his fingers, gave a sweet minty fragrance to the air between their faces—"that she might live."

The witch stood silent for a moment, while he felt his heart beating in the palms of his hands. "There is a gate in the hedge. Why did you not come through it, and knock on my door, and ask for what you need?"

"Because I was afraid," he murmured, and silence fell again.

"What ails the child?" the witch asked at last.

Hope flooded through him and made him tremble. "It is a wasting fever, and there is almost nothing of her left; often now she does not know us."

The witch turned away from him, and walked several steps; and he staggered to his feet, thinking to flee; but his head swam, and when it was clear, the witch stood again before him. She held a dark green frond out to him; its long, sharp leaves nodded over her hand, and the smell of it made his eyes water.

"Those leaves you wished to steal would avail you and your daughter little. They make a pleasant taste, steeped in hot water, and they give a fresh smell to linens long in a cupboard. Take this as my gift to your poor child; steep this in boiling water, and give it to the child to drink. She will not like it, but it will cure her; and you say she will die else."

The woodcutter looked in amazement at the harsh-smelling bough; and slowly he opened his fists, and the green leaves fell at his feet, and slowly he reached out for what the witch offered him. She was small of stature, he noticed suddenly, and slender, almost frail. She stooped as lithely as a maiden, and picked up the leaves he had dropped, and held them out to him.

"These too you shall keep, and boil as you meant to do,

for your child will need a refreshing draught after what you must give her for her life's sake.

"And you should at least have the benefit they can give you, for you shall pay a heavy toll for your thievery this night. Your wife carries your fifth child; in a little time, when your fourth daughter is well again, she shall tell you of it. In seven months she shall be brought to bed, and the baby will be big and strong. That child is mine; that child is the price you shall forfeit for this night's lack of courtesy."

"Ah, God," cried the woodcutter, "do you barter the death of one child against the death of another?"

"No," she said. "I give a life for a life. For your youngest child shall live; and the baby not yet born I shall raise kindly, for I"—she faltered—"I wish to teach someone my herb lore.

"Go now. Your daughter needs what you bring her." And the woodcutter found himself at the threshold of his own front door, his hands full of leaves, and his axe and yoke still deep in the forest; nor did he remember the journey home.

The axe and yoke were in their accustomed place the next morning; the woodcutter seized them up and strode into the forest by a path he knew would not take him near the witch's garden.

All four daughters were well and strong seven months later when their mother was brought to her fifth confinement. The birth was an easy one, and a fifth daughter kicked her way into the world; but the mother turned her face away, and the four sisters wept, especially the youngest. The midwife wrapped the baby up snugly in the birth clothes that had comforted four infants previously. The woodcutter picked up the child and went into the forest in the direction he had avoided for seven months. It had been in his heart since he had found himself on his doorstep with his hands full of leaves and unable to remember how he got there, that this journey was one he would not escape; so he held the child close to him, and went the shortest path he knew to the witch's garden. For all of its seven months' neglect, the way was as clear as when he had trodden it often.

This time he knocked upon the gate, and entered; the witch was standing before her front door. She raised her arms for the child, and the woodcutter laid her in them. The witch did not at first look at the baby, but rather up into the wood-cutter's face. "Go home to your wife, and the four daughters who love you, for they know you. And know this too: that in a year's time your wife shall be brought to bed once again, and the child shall be a son."

Then she bowed her head over the baby, and just before her black hair fell forward to hide her face, the woodcutter saw a look of love and gentleness touch the witch's sad eyes and mouth. He remembered that look often, for he never again found the witch's garden, though for many years he searched the woods where he knew it once had been, till he was no longer sure that he had ever seen it, and his family numbered four sons as well as four daughters.

Maugie named her new baby Erana. Erana was a cheerful baby and a merry child; she loved the garden that was her home; she loved Maugie, and she loved Maugie's son, Touk. She called Maugie by her name, Maugie, and not Mother, for Maugie had been careful to tell her that she was not her real mother; and when little Erana had asked, "Then why do I live with you, Maugie?" Maugie had answered: "Because I always wanted a daughter."

Touk and Erana were best friends. Erana's earliest memory was of riding on his shoulders and pulling his long pointed

81

ears, and drumming his furry chest with her small heels. Touk visited his mother's garden every day, bringing her wild roots that would not grow even in her garden, and split wood for her fire. But he lived by the riverbank, or by the pool that an elbow of the river had made. As soon as Erana was old enough to walk more than a few steps by herself, Touk showed her the way to his bit of river, and she often visited him when she could not wait for him to come to the garden. Maugie never went beyond her hedge, and she sighed the first time small Erana went off alone. But Touk was at home in the wild woods, and taught Erana to be at home there too. She lost herself only twice, and both those times when she was very small; and both times Touk found her almost before she had time to realize she was lost. They did not tell Maugie about either of these two incidents, and Erana never lost herself in the forest again.

Touk often took a nap at noontime, stretched out full length in his pool and floating three-quarters submerged; he looked like an old mossy log, or at least he did till he opened his eyes, which were a vivid shade of turquoise, and went very oddly with his green skin. When Erana first visited him, she was light enough to sit on his chest as he floated, and paddle him about like the log he looked, while he crossed his hands on his breast and watched her with a glint of blue between almost-closed green eyelids. But she soon grew too heavy for this amusement, and he taught her instead to swim, and though she had none of his troll blood to help her, still, she was a pupil to make her master proud.

One day as she lay, wet and panting, on the shore, she said to him, "Why do you not have a house? You do not spend all your hours in the water, or with us in the garden."

He grunted. He sat near her, but on a rough rocky patch

that she had avoided in favor of a grassy mound. He drew his knees up to his chin and put his arms around them. There were spurs at his wrists and heels, like a fighting cock's, and though he kept them closely trimmed, still he had to sit slightly pigeon-toed to avoid slashing the skin of his upper legs with the heel spurs, and he grasped his arms carefully well up near the elbow. The hair that grew on his head was as pale as young leaves, and inclined to be lank; but the tufts that grew on the tops of his shoulders and thickly across his chest, and the crest that grew down his backbone, were much darker, and curly.

"You think I should have a house, my friend?" he growled, for his voice was always a growl.

Erana thought about it. "I think you should *want* to have a house."

"I'll ponder it," he said, and slid back into the pool and floated out toward the center. A long-necked bird drifted down and landed on his belly, and began plucking at the ragged edge of one short trouser leg.

"You should learn to mend, too," Erana called to him. Erana loathed mending. The bird stopped pulling for a moment and glared at her. Then it reached down and raised a thread in its beak and wrenched it free with one great tug. It looked challengingly at Erana and then slowly flapped away, with the mud-colored thread trailing behind it.

"Then what would the birds build their nests with?" he said, and grinned. There was a gap between his two front teeth, and the eyeteeth curved well down over the lower lip.

Maugie taught her young protégé to cook and clean, and sew—and mend—and weed. But Erana had little gift for herb lore. She learned the names of things, painstakingly, and the by-rote rules of what mixtures did what and when;

but her learning never caught fire, and the green things in the garden did not twine lovingly around her when she paused near them as they seemed to do for Maugie. She learned what she could, to please Maugie, for Erana felt sad that neither her true son nor her adopted daughter could understand the things Maugie might teach; and because she liked to know the ingredients of a poultice to apply to an injured wing, and what herbs, mixed in with chopped-up bugs and earthworms, would make orphaned fledglings thrive.

For Erana's fifteenth birthday, Touk presented her with a stick. She looked at it, and then she looked at him. "I thought you might like to lay the first log of my new house," he said, and she laughed.

"You have decided then?" she asked.

"Yes; in fact I began to want a house long since, but I have only lately begun to want to build one," he said. "And then I thought I would put it off till your birthday, that you might make the beginning, as it was your idea first."

She hesitated, turning the little smooth stick in her hand. "It is—is it truly your idea now, Touk? I was a child when I teased you about your house; I would never mean to hold you to a child's nagging."

The blue eyes glinted. "It is my idea now, my dear, and you can prove that you are my dearest friend by coming at once to place your beam where it belongs, so that I may begin."

Birthdays required much eating, for all three of them liked to cook, and they were always ready for an excuse for a well-fed celebration; so it was late in the day of Erana's fifteenth birthday that she and Touk made their way—slowly, for they were very full of food—to his riverbank. "There," he said, pointing across the pool. Erana looked up at him question-ingly, and then made her careful way around the water to the stand of trees he had indicated; he followed on her heels. She stopped, and he said over her shoulder, his breath stir-ring her hair, "You see nothing? Here—" And he took her hand, and led her up a short steep slope, and there was a little clearing beyond the trees, with a high mossy rock at its back, and the water glinting through the trees before it, and the trees all around, and birds in the trees. There were al-ready one or two bird-houses hanging from suitable branches at the clearing's edge, and bits of twig sticking out the round doorways to indicate tenants in residence.

"My house will lie—" And he dropped her hand to pace off its boundaries; when he halted, he stood before her again, his blue eyes anxious for her approval. She bent down to pick up four pebbles; and she went solemnly to the four corners he had marked, and pushed them into the earth. He stood, watching her, at what would be his front door; and last she laid the stick, her birthday present, just before his feet. "It will be a lovely house," she said.

Touk's house was two years in the building. Daily Erana told Maugie how the work went forward: how there were to be five rooms, two downstairs and three above; how the frame jointed together; how the floor was laid and the roof covered it. How Touk had great care over the smallest detail: how not only every board slotted like silk into its given place, but there were little carven grinning faces peering out from the corners of cupboards, and wooden leaves and vines that at first glance seemed no more than the shining grain of the exposed wood, coiling around the arches of doorways. Touk built two chimneys, but only one fireplace. The other chim-ney was so a bird might build its nest in it.

"You must come see it," Erana said to her foster mother. "It is the grandest thing you ever imagined!" She could only say such things when Touk was not around, for Erana's praise of his handiwork seemed to make him uncomfortable, and he blushed, which turned him an unbecoming shade of violet.

Maugie laughed. "I will come when it is finished, to sit by the first fire that is laid in the new fireplace."

Touk often asked Erana how a thing should be done: the door here or there in a room, should the little face in this corner perhaps have its tongue sticking out for a change? Erana, early in the house building, began picking up the broken bits of trees that collected around Touk's work, and borrowed a knife, and began to teach herself to whittle. In two years' time she had grown clever enough at it that it was she who decorated the stairway, and made tall thin forest creatures of wood to stand upon each step and hold up the railing, which was itself a scaled snake with a benevolent look in his eye as he viewed the upper hallway, and a bird sitting on a nest in a curl of his tail instead of a newel post at the bottom of the staircase.

When Touk praised her work in turn, Erana flushed too, although her cheeks went pink instead of lavender; and she shook her head and said, "I admit I am pleased with it, but I could never have built the house. Where did you learn such craft?"

Touk scratched one furry shoulder with his nails, which curled clawlike over the tips of his fingers. "I practiced on my mother's house. My father built it; but I've put so many patches on it, and I've stared at its beams so often, that wood looks and feels to me as familiar as water."

Even mending seemed less horrible than usual, when the

86

tears she stitched together were the honorable tears of house building. Maugie was never a very harsh taskmaster and, as the house fever grew, quietly excused Erana from her lessons on herb lore. Erana felt both relieved and guilty as she noticed, but when she tried halfheartedly to protest, Maugie said, "No, no, don't worry about it. Time enough for such things when the house is finished." Erana was vaguely surprised, for even after her foster mother had realized that her pupil had no gift for it, the lessons had continued, earnestly, patiently, and a trifle sorrowfully. But now Maugie seemed glad, even joyful, to excuse her. Perhaps she's as relieved as I am, Erana thought, and took herself off to the riverbank again. She wished all the more that Maugie would come too, for she spent nearly all her days there, and it seemed unkind to leave her foster mother so much alone; but Maugie only smiled her oddly joyful smile, and hurried her on her way.

The day was chosen when the house was to be called complete; when Maugie would come to see the first fire laid—"And to congratulate the builder," Erana said merrily. "You will drown him in congratulations when you see."

"Builders," said Touk. "And I doubt the drowning."

Erana laughed. "Builder. And I don't suppose you *can* be drowned. But I refuse to argue with you; your mother knows us well enough to know which of us to believe."

Maugie smiled at them both.

Erana could barely contain her impatience to be gone as Maugie tucked the last items in the basket. This house feast would outdo all their previous attempts in that line, which was no small feat in itself; but Erana, for once in her life, was not particularly interested in food. Maugie gave them each their bundles to carry, picked up her basket, and looked around yet again for anything she might have forgotten.

"We'll close the windows first; it may rain," she said meditatively; Erana made a strangled noise and dashed off to bang sashes shut.

But they were on their way at last. Maugie looked around with mild surprise at the world she had not seen for so long.

"Have you never been beyond your garden?" Erana said curiously. "Were you born in that house?"

"No. I grew up far away from here. My husband brought me to this place, and helped me plant the garden; he built the house." Maugie looked sad, and Erana asked no more, though she had long wondered about Maugie's husband and Touk's father.

They emerged from the trees to the banks of Touk's river pool. He had cut steps up the slope to his house, setting them among the trees that hid his house from the water's edge, making a narrow twisting path of them, lined with flat rocks and edged with moss. Touk led the way.

The roof was steeply pitched, and two sharp gables struck out from it, with windows to light the second storey; the chimneys rose from each end of the house, and their mouths were shaped like wide-jawed dragons, their chins facing each other and their eyes rolling back toward the bird-houses hanging from the trees. And set all around the edges of the roof were narrow poles for more bird-houses, but Touk had not had time for these yet.

Touk smiled shyly at them. "It is magnificent," said his mother, and Touk blushed a deep violet with pleasure.

"Next I will lay a path around the edge of the pool, so that my visitors need not pick their way through brambles and broken rock." They turned back to look at the water, gleaming through the trees. Touk stood one step down, one hand on the young tree beside him, where he had retreated while he awaited his audience's reaction; and Maugie stood near him. As they were, he was only a head taller than she, and Erana noticed for the first time, as the late afternoon sun shone in their faces, that there was a resemblance between them. Nothing in feature perhaps, except that their eyes were set slanting in their faces, but much in expression. The same little half-smiles curled the corners of both their mouths at the moment, though Maugie lacked Touk's splendidly curved fangs.

"But I did not want to put off this day any longer, for today we can celebrate two things together."

"A happy birthday, Erana," said Maugie, and Erana blinked, startled.

"I had forgotten."

"You are seventeen today," Maugie said.

Erana repeated, "I had forgotten." But when she met Touk's turquoise eyes, suddenly the little smile left his face and some other emotion threatened to break through; but he dropped his eyes and turned his face away from her, and his hand trailed slowly down the bole of the tree. Erana was troubled and hurt, for he was her best friend, and she stared at his averted shoulder. Maugie looked from one to the other of them, and began to walk toward the house.

It was not as merry an occasion as it had been planned, for something was bothering Touk, and Erana hugged her hurt to herself and spoke only to Maugie. They had a silent, if vast, supper around the new-laid fire, sitting cross-legged on the floor, for Touk had not yet built any furniture. Maugie interrupted the silence occasionally to praise some detail she noticed, or ask some question about curtains or carpeting, which she had promised to provide. Her first gift to the new house already sat on the oak mantelpiece: a bowl of potpourri, which murmured through the sharper scents of the fire and the richer ones of the food.

Into a longer silence than most, Erana said abruptly, "This is a large house for only one man."

The fire snapped and hissed; the empty room magnified the sound so that they were surrounded by fire. Touk said, "Troll. One troll."

Erana said, "Your mother—"

"I am human, yes, but witch blood is not quite like other human blood," said Maugie.

"And I am my father's son anyway," said Touk. He stretched one hand out to the fire, and spread his fingers; they were webbed. The firelight shone through the delicate mesh of capillaries.

"Your father?"

"My father was a troll of the north, who—"

"Who came south for the love of a human witch-woman," said Maugie gravely.

Erana again did not ask a question, but the silence asked it for her. "He died thirty years ago; Touk was only four. Men found him, and . . . he came home to the garden to die." Maugie paused. "Trolls are not easily caught; but these men were poachers, and trolls are fond of birds. He lost his temper."

Touk shivered, and the curling hair down his spine erected and then lay flat again; Erana thought she would not wish to see him lose his temper. She said slowly, "And yet you stayed here."

"It is my home," Maugie said simply; "it is the place I was happy, and, remembering, I am happy again."

"And I have never longed for the sight of my own kind," said Touk, never raising his eyes from the fire. "I might have gone north, I suppose, when I was grown; but I would miss my river, and the birds of the north are not my friends."

Erana said, "My family?"

"You are a woodcutter's daughter," Maugie said, so quietly that Erana had to lean toward her to hear her over the fire's echoes. "I . . . did him a favor, but he, he had . . . behaved ill; and I demanded a price. My foster daughter, dearer than daughter, it was a trick and I acknowledge it. . . ."

She felt Maugie's head turn toward her, but Touk stared steadfastly at the hearth. "You always wanted a daughter," Erana said, her words as quiet as Maugie's had been, and her own eyes fixed on Maugie's son, who swallowed uncomfortably. "You wish that I should marry your son. This house he has built is for his wife."

Maugie put out a hand. "Erana, love, surely you—"

Touk said, "No, Mother, she has not guessed; has never guessed. I have seen that it has never touched her mind, for I would have seen if it had. And I would not be the one who forced her to think of it." Still he looked at the flames, and now, at last, Erana understood why he had not met her eyes that afternoon.

She stood up, looked blindly around her. "I—I must think."

Maugie said miserably, "Your family—they live in the village at the edge of the forest, south and east of here. He is the woodcutter; she bakes bread for the villagers. They have four daughters and four sons. . . ."

Erana found her way to the door, and left them.

Her feet took her back to the witch's garden, the home she had known for her entire life. She had wondered, fleetingly, once she understood that Maugie was not her mother, who her blood kin might be; but the question had never troubled her, for she was happy, loving and loved. It was twilight by the time she reached the garden; numbly she went to the house and fetched a shawl and a kerchief, and into the kerchief she put food, and then went back into the garden and plucked a variety of useful herbs, ones she understood, and tied the kerchief around them all. She walked out of the garden, and set her feet on a trail that no one had used since a woodcutter had followed it for the last time seventeen years before.

She walked for many days. She did not pause in the small village south and east of the witch's garden; she did not even turn her head when she passed a cottage with loaves of fresh bread on shelves behind the front windows, and the warm smell of the bread assailed her in the street. She passed through many other small villages, but she kept walking. She did not know what she sought, and so she kept walking. When she ran out of food, she did a little simple doctoring to earn more, and then walked on. It was strange to her to see faces that were not Maugie's or Touk's, for these were the only faces she had ever seen, save those of the forest beasts and birds; and she was amazed at how eagerly her simple herbcraft was desired by these strangers. She found some herbs to replace the ones she used in the fields and forests she passed, but the finest of them were in the garden she had left behind.

The villages grew larger, and became towns. Now she heard often of the king, and occasionally she saw a grand coach pass, and was told that only those of noble blood rode in such. Once or twice she saw the faces of those who rode within, but the faces looked no more nor less different from any of the other human faces she saw, although they wore more jewels.

Erana at last made her way to the capital city, but the city gates bore black banners. She wondered at this, and inquired of the gate guard, who told her that it was because the king's only son lay sick. And because the guard was bored, he told the small shabby pedestrian that the king had issued a proclamation that whosoever cured the prince should have the king's daughter in marriage, and half the kingdom.

"What is the prince's illness?" Erana asked, clutching her kerchief.

The guard shrugged. "A fever; a wasting fever. It has run many days now, and they say he cannot last much longer. There is no flesh left on his bones, and often he is delirious."

"Thank you," said Erana, and passed through the gates. She chose the widest thoroughfare, and when she had come some distance along it, she asked a passerby where the king's house lay; the woman stared at her, but answered her courteously.

The royal gate too was draped in black. Erana stood before it, hesitating. Her courage nearly failed her, and she turned to go, when a voice asked her business. She might still have not heeded it, but it was a low, growly, kind voice, and it reminded her of another voice dear to her; and so she turned toward it. A guard in a silver uniform and a tall hat smiled gently at her; he had young daughters at home, and he would not wish any of them to look so lost and worn and weary. "Do not be frightened. Have you missed your way?"

"N-no," faltered Erana. "I—I am afraid I meant to come to the king's house, but now I am not so sure."

"What is it the king or his guard may do for you?" rumbled the guard.

Erana blushed. "You will think it very presumptuous, but—but I heard of the prince's illness, and I have some . . . small . . . skill in healing." Her nervous fingers pulled her kerchief open, and she held it out toward the guard. The scent of the herbs from the witch's garden rose into his face and made him feel young and happy and wise.

He shook his head to clear it. "I think perhaps you have more than small skill," he said, "and I have orders to let all healers in. Go." He pointed the way, and Erana bundled her kerchief together again clumsily and followed his gesture.

The king's house was no mere house, but a castle. Erana had never seen anything like it before, taller than trees, wider than rivers; the weight of its stones frightened her, and she did not like walking up the great steps and under the vast stone archway to the door and the liveried man who stood beside it, nor standing in their gloom as she spoke her errand. The liveried man received her with more graciousness and less kindness than the silver guard had done, and he led her without explanation to a grand chamber where many people stood and whispered among themselves like a forest before a storm. Erana felt the stone ceiling hanging over her, and the stone floor jarred her feet. At the far end of the chamber was a dais with a tall chair on it, and in the chair sat a man.

"Your majesty," said Erana's guide, and bowed low; and Erana bowed as he had done, for she understood that one makes obeisance to a king, but did not know that women were expected to curtsey. "This . . . girl . . . claims to know something of leechcraft."

The whispering in the chamber suddenly stilled, and the air quivered with the silence, like the forest just before the first lash of rain. The king bent his heavy gaze upon his visitor, but when Erana looked back at him, his face was expressionless.

"What do you know of fevers?" said the king; his voice was as heavy as his gaze, and as gloomy as the stones of his castle, and Erana's shoulders bowed a little beneath it.

"Only a little, your majesty," she said, "but an herb I carry"—and she raised her kerchief—"does the work for me."

"If the prince dies after he suffers your tending," said the king in a tone as expressionless as his face, "you will die with him."

Erana stood still a moment, thinking, but her thoughts had been stiff and uncertain since the evening she had sat beside a first-laid fire in a new house, and the best they could do for her now was to say to her, "So?" Thus she answered: "Very well."

The king raised one hand, and another man in livery stepped forward, his footsteps hollow in the thick silence. "Take her to where the prince lies, and see that she receives what she requires and . . . do not leave her alone with him."

The man bowed, turned, and began to walk away; he had not once glanced at Erana. She hesitated, looking to the king for some sign; but he sat motionless, his gaze lifted from her and his face blank. Perhaps it is despair, she thought, almost hopefully: the despair of a father who sees his son dying. Then she turned to follow her new guide, who had halfway crossed the long hall while she stood wondering, and so she had to hasten after to catch him up. Over her soft footsteps she heard a low rustling laugh as the courtiers watched the country peasant run from their distinguished presence.

The guide never looked back. They came at last to a door

at which he paused, and Erana paused panting behind him. He opened the door reluctantly. Still without looking around, he passed through it and stopped. Erana followed him, and went around him, to look into the room.

It was not a large room, but it was very high; and two tall windows let the sunlight in, and Erana blinked, for the corridors she had passed through had been grey, stone-shadowed. Against the wall opposite the windows was a bed, with a canopy, and curtains pulled back and tied to the four pillars at its four corners. A man sat beside the bed, three more sat a little distance from it, and a man lay in the bed. His hands lay over the coverlet, and the fingers twitched restlessly; his lips moved without sound, and his face on the pillow turned back and forth.

Erana's guide said, "This is the latest . . . leech. She has seen the king, and he has given his leave." The tone of his voice left no doubt of his view of this decision.

Erana straightened her spine, and held up her bundle in her two hands. She turned to her supercilious guide and said, "I will need hot water and cold water." She gazed directly into his face as she spoke, while he looked over her head. He turned, nonetheless, and went out.

Erana approached the bed and looked down; the man sitting by it made no move to give her room, but sat stiffly where he was. The prince's face was white to the lips, and there were hollows under his eyes and cheekbones; and then, as she watched, a red flush broke out, and sweat stained his cheeks and he moaned.

The guide returned, bearing two pitchers. He put them on the floor, and turned to go. Erana said, "Wait," and he took two more steps before he halted, but he did halt, with his back to her as she knelt by the pitchers and felt the water within them. One was tepid; the other almost tepid. "This will not do," Erana said angrily, and the man turned around, as if interested against his will that she dared protest. She picked up the pitchers and with one heave threw their contents over the man who had fetched them. He gasped, and his superior look disappeared, and his face grew mottled with rage. "I asked for *hot* water and *cold* water. You will bring it, as your king commanded you to obey me. With it you will bring me two bowls and two cups. Go swiftly and return more swiftly. Go *now*." She turned away from him, and after a moment she heard him leave. His footsteps squelched.

He returned as quickly as she had asked; water still rolled off him and splashed to the floor as he moved. He carried two more pitchers; steam rose from the one, and dew beaded the other. Behind him a woman in a long skirt carried the bowls and cups.

"You will move away from the bed, please," Erana said, and the man who had not made room for her paused just long enough to prove that he paused but not so long as to provoke any reaction, stood up, and walked to the window. She poured some hot water into one bowl, and added several dark green leaves that had once been long and spiky but had become bent and bruised during their journey from the witch's garden; and she let them steep till the sharp smell of them hung like a green fog in the high-ceilinged room. She poured some of the infusion into a cup, and raised the prince's head from the pillow, and held the cup under his nostrils. He breathed the vapor, coughed, sighed; and his eyes flickered open. "Drink this," Erana whispered, and he bowed his head and drank.

She gave him a second cup some time later, and a third as

twilight fell; and then, as night crept over them, she sat at his bedside and waited, and as she had nothing else to do, she listened to her thoughts; and her thoughts were of Touk and Maugie, and of the king's sentence hanging over her head like the stone ceiling, resting on the prince's every shallow breath.

All that night they watched, and candlelight gave the prince's wan face a spurious look of health. But at dawn, when Erana stood stiffly and touched his forehead, it was cool. He turned a little away from her, and tucked one hand under his cheek, and lay quietly; and his breathing deepened and steadied into sleep.

Erana remained standing, staring dumbly down at her triumph. The door of the room opened, and her uncooperative guide of the day before entered, bearing on a tray two fresh pitchers of hot and cold water, and bread and cheese and jam and meat. Erana brewed a fresh minty drink with the cold water, and gave it to the prince with hands that nearly trembled. She said to the man who had been her guide, "The prince will sleep now, and needs only the tending that any patient nurse may give. May I rest?"

The man, whose eyes now dwelt upon her collarbone, bowed, and went out, and she followed him to a chamber not far from the prince's. There was a bed in it, and she fell into it, clutching her herb bundle like a pillow, and fell fast asleep.

She continued to assist in the tending of the prince since it seemed to be expected of her, and since she gathered that she should be honored by the trust in her skill she had so hardly earned. Within a fortnight the prince was walking, slowly but confidently; and Erana began to wonder how long she was expected to wait upon him, and then she wondered what she might do with herself once she was freed of that waiting.

There was no one at the court she might ask her questions. For all that she had been their prince's salvation, they treated her as distantly as they had from the beginning, albeit now with greater respect. She had received formal thanks from the king, whose joy at his son's health regained made no more mark on his expression and the tone of his voice than fear of his son's death had done. The queen had called Erana to her private sitting room to receive her thanks. The princess had been there too; she had curtseyed to Erana, but she had not smiled, any more than her parents had done.

And so Erana continued from day to day, waiting for an unknown summons; or perhaps for the courage to ask if she might take her leave.

A month after the prince arose from his sickbed he called his first Royal Address since his illness had struck him down. The day before the Address the royal heralds had galloped the royal horses through the streets of the king's city, telling everyone who heard them that the prince would speak to his people on the morrow; and when at noon on the next day he stood in the balcony overlooking the courtyard Erana had crossed to enter the palace for the first time, a mob of expectant faces tipped up their chins to watch him.

Erana had been asked to attend the royal speech. She stood in the high-vaulted hall where she had first met the king, a little behind the courtiers who now backed the prince, holding his hands up to his people, on the balcony. The king and queen stood near her; the princess sat gracefully at her ease in a great wooden chair lined with cushions a little distance from the open balcony. It seemed to Erana, she thought with some puzzlement, that they glanced at her often, although with their usual impassive expressions; and there was tension in the air that reminded her of the first time she had entered this hall, to tell the king that she knew a little of herbs and fevers.

Erana clasped her hands together. She supposed her special presence had been asked that she might accept some sort of royal thanks in sight of the people; she, the forest girl, who was still shy of people in groups. The idea that she might have to expose herself to the collective gaze of an audience of hundreds made her very uncomfortable; her clasped hands felt cold. She thought, It will please these people if I fail to accept their thanks with dignity, and so I shall be dignified. I will look over the heads of the audience, and pretend they are flowers in a field.

She did not listen carefully to what the prince was saying. She noticed that the rank of courtiers surrounding the prince had parted, and the king stepped forward as if to join his son on the balcony. But he paused beside Erana, and seized her hands, and led or dragged her beside him; her hands were pinched inside his fingers, and he pulled at her awkwardly, so that she stumbled. They stood on the balcony together, and she blinked in the sunlight; she looked at the prince, and then turned her head back to look at the king, still holding her hands prisoned as if she might run away. She did not look down, at the faces beyond the balcony.

"I offered my daughter's hand in marriage and half my kingdom to the leech who cured my son." The king paused, and a murmur, half surprise and half laughter, wrinkled the warm noontide air. He looked down at Erana, and still his face was blank. "I wish now to adjust the prize and payment for the service done me and my people and my kingdom: my son's hand in marriage to the leech who saved him, and beside him, the rule of all my kingdom."

The prince reached across and disentangled one of her hands from his father's grip, so that she stood stretched between them, like game on a pole brought home from the hunt. The people in the courtyard were shouting; the noise hurt her head, and she felt her knees sagging, and the pull on her hands, and then a hard grip on her upper arms to keep her standing; and then all went black.

She came to herself lying on a sofa. She could hear the movements of several people close beside her, but she was too tired and troubled to wish to open her eyes just yet on the world of the prince's betrothed; and so she lay quietly.

"I think they might have given her some warning," said one voice. "She does have thoughts of her own."

A laugh. "Does she? What makes you so sure? A little nobody like this—I'm surprised they went through with it. She's not the type to insist about anything. She creeps around like a mouse, and never speaks unless spoken to. Not always then."

"She spoke up for herself to Roth."

"Roth is a fool. He would not wear the king's livery at all if his mother were not in waiting to the queen . . . . And she's certainly done nothing of the sort since. Give her a few copper coins and a new shawl . . . and a pat on the head . . . and send her on her way."

"She did save the prince's life."

A snort. "I doubt it. Obviously the illness had run its course; she just happened to have poured some ridiculous quack remedy down his throat at the time."

There was a pause, and then the first voice said, "It is a pity she's so plain. One wants a queen to set a certain standard. . . ."

Erana shivered involuntarily, and the voice stopped abruptly. Then she moaned a little, as if only just coming to consciousness, and opened her eyes.

Two of the queen's ladies-in-waiting bent over her. She recognized the owner of the second voice immediately from the sour look on her face. The kindlier face said to her, "Are you feeling a little better now? May we bring you anything?"

Erana sat up slowly. "Thank you. Would you assist me to my room, please?"

She easily persuaded them to leave her alone in her own room. At dinnertime a man came to inquire if she would attend the banquet in honor of the prince's betrothal? She laughed a short laugh and said that she felt still a trifle overcome by the news of the prince's betrothal, and desired to spend her evening resting quietly, and could someone perhaps please bring her a light supper?

Someone did, and she sat by the window watching the twilight fade into darkness, and the sounds of the banquet far away from her small room drifting up to her on the evening breeze. I have never spoken to the prince alone, she thought; I have never addressed him but as a servant who does what she may for his health and comfort; nor has he spoken to me but as a master who recognizes a servant who has her usefulness.

Dawn was not far distant when the betrothal party ended. She heard the last laughter, the final cheers, and silence. She sighed and stood up, and stretched, for she was stiff with sitting. Slowly she opened the chest where she kept her herb kerchief and the shabby clothes she had travelled in. She laid aside the court clothes she had never been comfortable in, for all that they were plain and simple compared with those the others wore, and dressed herself in the skirt and blouse that she and Maugie had made. She ran her fingers over the patches in the skirt that house building had caused. She hesitated, her bundle in hand, and then opened another, smaller chest, and took out a beautiful shawl, black, embroidered in red and gold, and with a long silk fringe. This she folded gently, and wrapped inside her kerchief.

Touk had taught her to walk quietly, that they might watch birds in their nests without disturbing them, and creep close to feeding deer. She slipped into the palace shadows, and then into the shadows of the trees that edged the courtyard; once she looked up, over her shoulder, to the empty balcony that opened off the great hall. The railings of the ornamental fence that towered grandly over the gate and guardhouse were set so far apart that she could squeeze between them, pulling her bundle after her.

She did not think they would be sorry to see her go; she could imagine the king's majestic words: *She has chosen to decline the honor we would do her, feeling herself unworthy; and having accepted our grateful thanks for her leechcraft, she has withdrawn once again to her peaceful country obscurity. Our best wishes go with her.* . . . But still she walked quietly, in the shadows, and when dawn came, she hid under a hedge in a garden, and slept, as she had often done before. She woke up once, hearing the hoofs of the royal heralds rattle past; and she wondered what news they brought. She fell asleep again, and did not waken till twilight; and then she crept out and began walking again.

She knew where she was going this time, and so her journey back took less time than her journey away had done.

Still she was many days on the road, and since she found that her last experience of them had made her shy of humankind, she walked after sunset and before dawn, and followed the stars across open fields instead of keeping to the roads, and raided gardens and orchards for her food, and did not offer her skills as a leech for an honest meal or bed.

The last night she walked into the dawn and past it, and the sun rose in the sky, and she was bone-weary and her feet hurt, and her small bundle weighed like rock. But here was her forest again, and she could not stop. She went past Maugie's garden, although she saw the wisp of smoke lifting from the chimney, and followed the well-known track to Touk's pool. She was too tired to be as quiet as she should be, and when she emerged from the trees, there was nothing visible but the water. She looked around and saw that Touk had laid the path around the shore of the pool that he had promised, and now smooth grey stones led the way to the steep steps before Touk's front door.

As she stood at the water's edge, her eyes blurred, and her hands, crossed over the bundle held to her breast, fell to her sides. Then there was a commotion in the pool, and Touk stood up, water streaming from him, and a strand of waterweed trailing over one pointed ear. Even the center of the pool for Touk was only thigh-deep, and he stood, riffling the water with his fingers, watching her.

"Will you marry me?" she said.

He smiled, his lovely, gap-toothed smile, and he blinked his turquoise eyes at her, and pulled the waterweed out of his long hair.

"I came back just to ask you that. If you say no, I will go away again."

"No," he said. "Don't go away. My answer is yes."

And he waded over to the edge of the pool and seized her in his wet arms and kissed her; and she threw her arms eagerly around his neck, and dropped her bundle. It opened in the water like a flower, and the herbs floated away across the surface, skittering like water bugs; and the embroidered silk shawl sank to the bottom.

Buttercups

There was an old farmer who married a young wife. He had been married once before, in his own youth, but his wife had died of a fever after they had been together only a year. In his grief the farmer forgot about all other human creatures and set himself only to his farm; and because there was both strength and fire in him, his farm bloomed and blossomed, and he himself did not know that his heart held its winter about it.

But all winters end, and the farmer's heart was secretly warm within its winter, and one day it melted: at the sight of a young girl at the town well. The girl was nothing like his first wife; it was not memories she aroused, but something new. Some green spring woke in him in a moment, and yet he had had no warning of it. He thought that he felt no different than he had for twenty years; that the coldness under his breastbone was an old scar, with nothing living and stirring beneath it; that some things only came once in a man's life.

And yet it was not the girl herself that had first caught his eye, but her horse. He was driving in to market as he did at this time every week, from spring through autumn, and his road lay past the town well, where there were very often people. Sometimes there were people he knew, and he would speak to them as he passed; for he seldom paused. But this day the well was almost deserted, and his eye swept over it and made to go on, but for the curve of a chestnut neck and the prance of chestnut forelegs. A beautiful young mare, he thought, looking at her appreciatively, with a sparkle to her and a kind eye. And then his eye was distracted, and then caught firmly, by a long chestnut braid of human hair falling over a human shoulder, as the girl bent to reach her brimming bucket. And she glanced up at the sound of the farmer's wagon wheels, and their eyes met, and she smiled.

He could not think of anything but how he would see her again. He was a polite man, and he knew nothing of this girl; he knew he should not have stopped or spoken, but he did both. He had enough sense remaining to him not to ask bluntly and immediately what her name was and where she lived; but he was unaccustomed to making conversation at any time, the use of speech was reserved for weather, crops, prices, and occasionally health; and he was confused and distressed by his own wish to speak to this girl he knew nothing of, but that she was as beautiful in her way as her mare, and had as kind an eye. Awkwardly he offered what he might have said to an acquaintance he had no immediate business with, that it was a fine morning, wasn't it, preventing himself with some difficulty from jumping down from his wagon and helping her with her water bucket, which she needed no help with. She fastened it to a knot on her saddle-skirt with a deftness of long practice that he knew he could not have matched, even had he been able to recognize how it fastened at all; and he watched her take down the long thin-lidded bucket from the other side of the saddle and dip it in its turn. He was dumbly grateful for the extra moments of her company, but desire to make a good impression and frustration at his inability to think of a way to do so made his hands close anxiously on his own reins, till the placid beast between the shafts of his wagon put its ears back and shook its head to remind him of its existence.

She agreed that it was a fine morning, but went on, easily, as if conversation with tongue-tied old men were pleasant and natural and ordinary, almost as if she were as glad of him as he was of her, that the land here was so much different from the mountains to which she was accustomed that all weathers seemed to lie differently against her skin; that a really fine day here in the lowlands seemed to go on forever because you could see so far away. The farmer, bemused by such richness of response to his gruff opening, grasped at an opportunity as it sailed by and said that he had not seen her before. No; she was recently come with her parents and younger brothers and sisters; but they had been travelling for some time, and everyone liked this town, and her father had been offered work almost at once, and so they thought they would stay for a time.

The farmer breathed a sigh. "I will look for you next market day," he said, daring greatly, and then added nervously, "If I may."

"Thank you," she said, and without any sign of awareness that she was saying something bold or over-friendly, added straightforwardly: "I will like recognizing a face in the crowds here. I am not used to so large a town."

The farmer worked no less hard than usual over the next

weeks, but it was a fortunate thing that he had farmed so long and well that his hands and back and feet and eyes knew what to do with little help from his brain, for all he could think of was the girl he had met at the town well, and of the next time he would see her. He held to his own standards, blindly, like clinging to a rock in a storm; he had gone to town once a week for the last twenty years, and he went on going into town once a week. But he could not have stayed away, that one day each week, had his house been on fire as he set his horse trotting down the road toward the next meeting with the girl he had seen at the well.

Her name was Coral, and she had four brothers and sisters, and a mother and father; but he barely noticed these. He did notice that he was not the only man who had noticed Coral, and that often when he found her, she was talking to young men who smiled at her as he could not, with the confidence of youth and charm, and swaggered when they walked. This made him wild, in his stiff and quiet way, but there was nothing he had any right to say or do about whom she chose to talk to; and he knew this, and held his peace. And she always had time for him, time to talk to him; the young men vanished when she turned to him, and he did not know if this was a good thing or a bad.

Usually they met at the well, as they had the first time; at first he did not think about this, beyond straining his eyes looking for her as soon as he could begin to differentiate the smaller hump of well from the bigger humps of buildings on the road into town. But on the fourth week he was a little delayed in setting out by a loose horseshoe, and his wagon-horse was too sober an animal to respond favorably to any nonsense about hurrying once they were on their way. And when they pulled up by the well, each a bit cross and breathless with resisting the other's will, the farmer realized that Coral was not merely there, as if perhaps she too had been delayed, but appeared to be *still* there, fiddling unconvincingly with a harness strap, her color a little heightened, and for the first time she seemed not completely at her ease with him. Almost she succeeded in sounding casual when she told him that after she fetched water on market days, and took the buckets home, she went on to the market itself, where she would spend most of the rest of the morning.

This made the farmer thoughtful. He was not late again at the well for the next several weeks, but having let a week go by, to maintain the pretense of casualness, a fortnight after Coral told him about her market-day mornings, he left the stall he shared with several other local farmers when it was his turn for a break, and went purposefully looking for her. His stall was away from the central marketplace, because at this time of year it specialized in the sort of produce only other farmers were much interested in. He found her easily in the bustling square where all the townsfolk were; he found her as if she were the only thing his eyes could rest on in all the hurry and hubbub. And that she was glancing around herself, over each shoulder, restlessly, even hopefully, might only have been that she was not pleased with the greens that were heaped up in the stall before her, and was wondering if better might be had nearby.

His own lack of imagination shocked him: How could he not have thought of doing this before? She had mentioned that she did much of the shopping for her family, that her mother was not good at it at all, although the sister next to her in age showed some promise and her brother Rack was the deadliest person she'd ever seen in pursuit of a bargain. Why had she lingered at the well, hoping to meet an old man with little conversation and no imagination?

The week after that he met the sister next in age, Moira, and Rack, who looked at him measuringly; but it was only Coral's opinion that mattered to him, and he greeted them politely but without much attention. The week after that he found her alone again, bending over Met's lettuces; Met, hovering in the back of the stall, was watching her with the expression of a hawk watching a young rabbit. Without thinking about it—and so giving him the opportunity to talk himself out of it—he walked up to her and put his hand gently but inexorably under her elbow and led her away. "Even your brother Rack would have a little trouble with Met," he explained; "the best of Met's energy has always gone into arguing, not into farming."

"Thank you," she said, looking into his eyes, her forearm resting warmly but without weight against the palm of his hand. "I did not think I liked what I was seeing and hearing, but I had not yet made up my mind. I find the people here much as I find the weather: like and unlike what I am used to, and I am not always sure I am reading the signs aright." And she smiled at him.

On the tenth week he asked her to marry him.

He had not meant to ask; it was not in his conscious mind to ask. But he missed her so, those long weeks on the farm, with no one to talk to but his horses and cows and chickens and sheep, and Turney the dog, and Med and Thwan, who were good workers—he would not have had anyone who was not—but who were perhaps even less talkative than he was himself. He had not realized, before he met Coral, that he missed conversation with other human beings. He would have said he did not miss conversations with other human beings; he only missed Coral.

He was appalled at what he had done when he heard in his own ears what his tongue had betrayed him by saying; but he was struck dumb with it, and so there was time for Coral to say, "Yes, Pos, please, I should like to marry you."

His mouth fell open; he shut it again. After a moment he reached out and clumsily took her hand, and she put her other hand on top of his. She looked at him, smiling a little, but the smile was hesitant. "If you did not mean it, I will let you off," she said after a moment, when he remained mute. "It is only that I—I would like to marry you. I have been hoping you would ask me."

He kissed her then, so that conversation was not necessary, for he thought he still could not speak; but that first touch of her lips against his made the possibility of speech flee even further. But he thought, deep in his heart, of all the long days and evenings at the farm, working side by side, when they could talk or not as they wished; when he might be able to kiss her for no reason at all, familiarly, because he wanted to, because she was his wife, because she was there. And he smiled as he kissed her, and kissed her again.

She stopped him as he would have kissed her a third time and said, "Wait. One thing you must know. I have no dowry; there are five of us, you know, and I'm the eldest; I know there's none to spare now; by the time Elana grows up perhaps there will be a little to be squeezed out, although I don't know, there may be a sixth and a seventh by then. My father earns little, and this will not change, there are only so many hours in a day, and he gets tired, and my mother . . . well,

115

never mind. Moly is mine—that is my mare—and I will bring her—that is, I hope you will let me bring her; she is a dear friend, I could not bear to sell her—but she is a riding horse, and I am afraid you will think she is a silly creature to have on a farm."

"I do not care about your dowry," said Pos then, finding his tongue in his need to reassure his beloved. "I love you, and that is what I care about, and my farm is big enough to support a wife—it is a family farm, it has been my family's farm through four generations. The house has rooms enough inside, and land enough outside; it goes to waste, with me alone. Of course Moly is welcome too." And then he said, from the fullness of his heart, "Thank you."

Coral sighed, and put her head on his shoulder, and then he drew her to one side where they could sit on a hay bale that was part of the rough partitions between stall and stall in the market, where they could talk quietly and ignore the world and be happy, and Pos thought he had never known anything like the contentment of Coral's side pressed against his, that no two people had ever fit together so comfortably as she in the curve of his arm. They stayed this way till it was time for him to go; she told him she would give the news to her family in her own way. "When . . . will I see you again?" he said, stammering a little, trying not to sound pathetic; would she hold him to their weekly visits, even now?

But she smiled at him, smiled a long warm smile the like of which he had never seen on her face before, and answered, "How I have wished that your market days came oftener than once a week! And how embarrassed I have been for thinking so, you with your farm to tend, and an honest hard-working man as you are! You may see me again as soon as you like. Tomorrow?''

And so for one week he came to the town three times. On the first visit he asked her to marry him, and on the second he was congratulated (noisily) by her family, and met her parents for the first time, a small faded father with deep lines in his face, a charming but vague mother. He noticed without noticing—for he could think of nothing clearly but his Coral—that it seemed to be Coral and the next-oldest girl, Moira, and the younger son, Rack, who knew where things were in the small drab house at the edge of town, who made the guest comfortable and laid the table for a meal. The elder son, Del, looked as faded and vague as his parents, but the baby, Elana, was as bright and sharp as her sisters. All this passed through his mind without lodging there, and he gave himself up to the celebration that grew so lively that even Del and the father laughed and moved a little more quickly.

And on his third visit to town that week he and Coral were married, and he took her home to his farm, which she had never seen, though it was near the town; and behind the wagon, in which Coral's small bundle of belongings rode, trotted Moly, the chestnut mare.

Coral was a good worker; she worked as hard as Pos did himself, and seemed to think of no other life, and Pos was happier than he had ever imagined. He had long thought that happiness had nothing to do with him, and what had to do with him was work. He had thought he had been satisfied with work; and he had been, for his heart had been held in its winter, and he had imagined nothing else, certainly not the transformation that happiness brings, so that

117

the very definitions of *work* and *satisfaction* are changed. Waking in the morning and finding Coral next to him gave him a shock of joy each day, and he got out of bed smiling, he who had been slow and grumbling in the mornings for the long years of his solitude.

He told her this—for he found that he could tell her almost anything, that things that he had failed to find words for even to explain to himself fell into place and sense when he opened his mouth to Coral—and she teased him, saying it was only because he had never learned to eat a proper breakfast. By the time he came downstairs these mornings, shaved and dressed, she, her hair still pillow-mussed and her nightclothes still on, had made what she considered a proper breakfast: porridge with beans or lentils in it, pancakes from potatoes left of last night's supper or chopped hash from last night's roast. He washed up as she dressed, and they went into the fields together.

They had gone into the fields together, naturally, without a word said on either side, from the first morning. Pos thought nothing but of the pleasure of her company, and willingly helped her in the evenings sweep the floor and get supper. He was a tidy man, and had kept house for himself for twenty years, since his mother died of grief after his father's early death; without thinking of it, perhaps he remembered his parents, knew that he had wanted a wife again because he wanted a companion. He would have missed her if she had stayed in the house all day, as he had missed her when she was in town all week; and they worked side by side in the fields as they did laundry side by side one morning a week in the house. He did not measure her help in terms of how many rows she hoed, or whether the shelves of the house were more or less dusty than they had been before two people lived there again, but only in the deliciousness of joined lives. He could think of his first wife again for the first time since he had lost her; and he remembered her sadly, both for the life she had not lived to spend and for the life they would have had together, for she was a tenderer creature than Coral, and there had never been any possibility of her working as he worked.

So the months passed, and the seed went into the ground and began to come up first as tiny green pinpricks and then as stout green stalks, and calves and chicks and lambs were born and ran around as young things do, and Turney shepherded everyone carefully and soberly whether they wanted to be shepherded or not. And Pos discovered that there were, in fact, two holes in the close weave of his happiness.

He saw the first as a result of overhearing a conversation between Med and Thwan.

He had merely assumed some increase in his plans for his farm with Coral's coming, and had never thought of or suggested to Med and Thwan any end of the work they did for him. When he found out what Coral could do and wanted to do, he would know how to plan properly for next year; this year would come as it came. That this was unlike him he knew, but his joy in his new wife made him misjudge just how out of character it was, and how it might look to the men who had worked with him for over a decade. If he thought about their reaction to Coral at all, he dismissed it by thinking that she was none of their business, and further, he did not believe either of them to be spiteful.

"—don't like it," Med was saying.

"We can hope for the best till we know the worst," Thwan replied, shortly, as if he wished the conversation at an end.

"She only married him to get away from her family, know this," Med went on, with a curious passion in his voice. "Five of them and a shiftless mother, and the father works only as much as he must. She'll weary of farm life soon enough."

"We don't know that," said Thwan. "She's a good worker."

"She is now," said Med. "She's only just come, thinking to be happy with her bargain."

"She's that pretty," said Thwan. "She need not have married Pos. She might have had half the young men in town."

"None of the young men have holdings half so grand as Pos's farm," said Med. "She's a wandering gnast's daughter; the young men who make up to her are not likely to offer anything near as good as marriage and land. Her family's moved on already, did you know that? Her father didn't even finish his last job. Unloaded her and got out of town. They'll have left debts that Pos'll have to pay. You wait and see."

"Stop it," said Thwan.

"And her out in the fields every day, so he can see her, looking over her shoulder to be sure he's watching, seeing what a good wife he's got, showing off, getting her hands dirty, as if that makes her a farmer," said Med, as if he couldn't stop.

"She need not be like her family, and that be no part of the reason why she took Pos, and fond of him she is, I believe," said Thwan, "and the sweat runs down her face as it does ours, and I've seen blisters on her hands. That's the last of it, Med, I say, and I will listen to no more."

Pos had come into the barn to speak to Thwan, but had stopped upon hearing their voices, the old reflex of silence coming back to him unthinking; or perhaps it was surprise at surprising them at so unusual an occupation as conversation; or perhaps it was only courtesy, not to interrupt what did not include him. At Thwan's final statement he turned and left, without letting them know of his presence, telling himself that it was that he wished not to embarrass them, Med particularly, who was only being loyal to a master (Pos told himself) he also considered a friend, telling himself that he would not think further about what they had said.

But he did think of it; he could not help himself. When he reached out, in the early morning, to stroke Coral's cheek to wake her—for it was always he who opened his eyes first— he saw his old gnarled hand against her smooth young skin, and sometimes he could not bear it, and drew back without touching her, and spoke her name instead. These moments did not—had not—lingered in his memory, or so he believed, because always she turned, still half asleep, and put an arm around his neck to pull his face down to hers that she might kiss him; that was what he remembered. But those moments he had chosen to forget rushed back to him upon Med's words, those moments in the early morning and many others, for suddenly there were many others, and he stood still again, having broken his promise not to think about what he had heard before he even had left the barn, and drew his breath as if it hurt him.

The second thing had not troubled him until the first gave him the opportunity his fears had been seeking to break out of their dungeons and torment him.

His farm had been his father's farm, and his father's, and his before him. His family seemed to have farming in its blood, for the farm had done well for four generations, from that first great-grandfather who knew where to take up the first spadeful of earth to begin a farm; and each son had been as eager as the father to tend the good land. Each generation had pushed the wild country back a little, claiming a little more pasture and cropland from wilderness, though each generation knew the wilderness was there, just beyond their last fences, leaning over the last furrowed rows, short-lived thorn and bramble and the shadows of oaks hundreds of years old. This did not trouble the farmers; the wild land was the wild land, and they had their farm, and one was one and the other was the other.

Pos's farm was roughly a square. The land here was almost flat, and since there was plenty of water, there was no reason to follow one line over another, and so as each farmer laid out his extra field, he tended to measure from the center, where the farmhouse and barns were (the house was a little nearer one edge of the square, where what had become the road to what had become the town was). The fields were not perfectly regular; there was a little contour to the ground that was worth following. But the lines were still quite recognizably close to straight.

Except for one corner. There was a squiggle in one corner, a hummock-shaped squiggle, a big hummock, with roots, like a big tree, and the roots ran into the carefully tended farm fields, like an underground ripple. This hummock was low itself, though visible enough in a terrain almost flat, and it was covered with low scrubby underbrush; and behind it was a tiny concavity of valley, a cup within its ring. Altogether the hummock, its roots, and its valley were perhaps the size of one good generous pasture for a modest herd of cows.

This hummock refused to be cultivated. Pos had never

tried, because his father and grandfather had told him it was not worth it; nothing would grow there but weeds and wildflowers. They and their father and grandfather had tried clearing and planting it, and for one season it remained barren, while the sowed seed refused to sprout, and the second season saw the wilderness return. Trees never grew there, and the scrub never took over, the way scrub usually did on neglected meadows; chiefly what the hummock was was a haven for wildflowers.

There were wildflowers everywhere, of course, for the ground was rich and the summers long and warm. Buttercups sprang up in the little deer-browsed meadows scattered among the trees in the long level spaces beyond the farm, buttercups and daisies, the big yellow and white and yellow and brown daisies, and the tiny pale pink and white ones; and cow parsley and poppies and meadowsweet and forget-me-nots and violets and heartsease, and dandelions, dandelions could grow anywhere. All these seeded the wind and sank their tiny stubborn roots on Pos's farm as well, where they were furrowed under or plucked up. Poppies occasionally sprang up behind the deep cut of the plough blade. But in general the wildflowers stayed beyond the confines of the farm and looked on politely, with the thorn and scrub and grasses and saplings and big old trees, and there was some of one and some of another, and the ordinary balance of uncultivated land stretched untroublingly before the eye.

The hillock was drowned in buttercups. The occasional daisy grew there, too, and nothing would keep out dandelions; but it was the buttercups that reigned, sun-bright from early May till the end of September, their tangled stems thick as weaving. Pos had always had a faint nagging feeling about the hillock; there was something not right about it, that great hot swath of yellow, it didn't look natural, it unsettled the eye, his eye. He felt there was something he ought to do about it—something besides the straightforward razing and planting that his forebears had proved did not work—but he had plenty to occupy him in the rest of his farm, and so he left it alone, carrying the small nagging feeling with him the best he could.

But Coral loved the little wild hillock. The first buttercups of the year were coming out when he brought his bride to the farm; they caught her eye at once, and immediately she named it Buttercup Hill. "But they are not buttercups, you know," she said, the first time she walked there. He had taken her all around the farm, showing her everything, even the corners of the barns where old tools lay, broken since his grandfather's day and never thrown out, because as soon as something is thrown out, there is some bit of it that might have been salvaged and used. He took her all around his fields, even to the edge of the small wild hillock.

He had not wanted to go any farther; he preferred to keep his feet on farmland. But the story of it intrigued her, and she would go, and he had gone with her because he had to, or lose the pleasure of her arm through his, and he was not willing to do that unnecessarily, even for a moment. He thought he could bear it for a moment or two, for the sake of keeping her at his side.

But she looked at the ground curiously as they walked up the little slope, and pawed as a horse might at the little yellow flowers that were already blooming thick and plentiful despite the earliness of the season. And then she bent and plucked one of them up. "These aren't buttercups, whatever your great-great-grandfather called them. Buttercups don't grow like this, for one thing—their stems mostly run around underground, not on top in a mat—and the flowers are the wrong shape, although I give you that they're the right size and color, and at a distance you wouldn't guess." She frowned at the flower she held, but in a friendly fashion, and spun its stem in her fingers. "I have no idea what they are, though. I know wildflowers pretty well, but these are new to me. Your lowlands are a strange country, dear Pos."

And she loved Buttercup Hill all the more as the riot of yellow gained strength in the summer heat. Pos said to her once that he did not like the unbroken fury of yellow upon that hill, and she laughed at him, and called him Old Grumbler. She said that she would make him a yellow shirt—just that buttercup yellow, to smite his dull eye—and he would wear it (she said, she would make him wear it if she had to), and he would learn about brightness and color, and that not everything had to be brown and green and grow in rows, and he would be so astonished that he would have to give up grumbling. He had laughed with her, and said that he would merely find something else to grumble about, old habits died hard. Yes, yes, she said, she was sure he could find other things to grumble about, why didn't he begin to make a list so that she could get started quickly, thinking of ways to foil everything on it, it would give them something to do during the long winter evenings, grumbling and foiling. And that summer evening ended in making love, as many of their evenings did. But Pos's small nagging feeling about Buttercup Hill grew no less persistent.

There was one thing he and Coral did not do together, and that was her afternoon ride. She did not have time for it every day, but she had Moly to exercise, and she loved her young mare too, and so most days she found time. Sometimes she worked so quickly—so as not to feel she was not doing her share, she said—that Pos remonstrated with her, telling her she did not need to exhaust herself, that he did not begrudge her an hour for her horse. She teased him about this too, saying that they should buy him a riding horse, that he could come with her; but he used those hours to poke into corners, in the house, the barns, the fields, to see if there was anything he had overlooked that should not be overlooked, and heard what she was saying as teasing only. He could sit on a horse, but riding gave him no particular pleasure; none of his family had ever been riders; there was no need for a farmer to be a horse rider.

Coral was out riding the afternoon that he overheard the conversation between Med and Thwan.

Coral almost always rode to Buttercup Hill and—she said—had a good gallop around the valley before turning for home, Moly trotting politely along the neat paths through the farm fields.

It was as if Med's words shone a great bright light in the corner of Pos's mind where he had banished (he thought) what was only a small nagging feeling. And the new light threw shadows from thoughts he had not known were there at all; he had done more banishing than he let himself remember. Did Coral not like farm life? Had he always suspected this? Did she like the hillock for its wildness—not because it was a good place to gallop her mare but because the farm fields constricted her, made her restless? He had seen no sign of it—he thought. But—he believed in her sense of honor as he could not quite believe in her love for him. It was reasonable—reasonable—that she should want to escape from her chaotic family, her vague parents, and their dingy lives; it was more than reasonable that she should prefer an offer of marriage to an offer of dalliance.

That did not mean that she loved him. That she wanted him and his farm.

He could bear that, he thought, carefully, coldly. But he did not think he could bear to lose her.

What could he offer her but stability? Stability was little enough to a young and beautiful woman; little enough after the first satisfied flush of having achieved a clever thing has worn off. He was not a wealthy man, and almost everything he earned he put back into his farm; no other way had ever occurred to him, it was what his family had always done. He remembered their conversation about the yellow shirt Coral had said she would make him; remembered it with pain, now, remembered how that evening had ended as if he had already lost her. His house—their house—was as plain as he was; where there were carpets on the floor they were there for warmth, not beauty; where there were cushions on the chairs they were there for comfort only, the patterns so faded he could not see them, and so old he could not remember them. The chairs themselves were square and functional— and plain—like the rooms, like the house, like the farm, like himself.

It was that same afternoon that she said to him, "I have noticed a curious thing: Moly's shoes turn yellow—yellow as buttercups—when we're riding through Buttercup Hill. And horseshoe-colored again as soon as we leave."

He had not meant to go to meet her; his feet had taken him toward her without his conscious volition; he wanted the nearness of her, the fact of her warmth and her self, the comfort of her existence in his trouble—for all that his trouble was about her, about losing the having of her. He had looked up to the clatter of hoofs and seen her coming toward him, the mare's mane and her braid blowing back in the wind of their motion. She stopped beside him and said, "Come up behind me. You can put your foot in the stirrup—I'll kick this one loose." He shook his head, still deep in unhappy reflections, the sight of her only making them more acute.

"Oh, Pos, one of your moods of gloom? Have you been out with your measuring stick—when you could be out galloping with the wind in your face—have you discovered the wheat is half a finger's breadth shorter than it should be at this season? Let me distract you. I have noticed a curious thing—" And she told him.

"At first I thought I was imagining it—of course. It was a trick of the light, or pollen, or something; or even some odd characteristic of your lowland blacksmiths' metal. But today I dismounted and picked Moly's feet up and looked at her shoes—and they were *yellow*. Yellow as gold. It even felt different, those yellow horseshoes, when I touched them. Softer. And," she went on as if the end of her tale was as interesting as the beginning, "do you know, the flower stems of your funny not-buttercups are so dense you really don't touch the earth itself at all now? I should have been worried about Moly's getting her feet caught, I think, earlier in the year, but I certainly don't have to now."

At the word *gold* Pos did look up at her, and when she came to the end of her story, she leaned down and grasped his hair, close to the scalp, and tipped his head farther back. "I cannot have a conversation with you down there and me up here. If you will not come up, I will have to get down, and then Moly will feel cheated. As will I, if you don't say something soon."

He could not stop himself smiling at her then, looking into her face smiling at him; he loved her so, and her presence felt like—like sunlight, and himself some slip of a seedling. "There, that's better," she said.

"If I get up behind you, Moly will feel worse than cheated," he said. "I am no lightweight."

"It will be good for her," said Coral, and pulled her foot free of the stirrup. "She has not enough challenges in her life. It is why I want to teach you to ride too; Moly would like another horse to run with. Have you seen her cavorting around your old plough horses, biting their withers, trying to get them to play with her?"

He, sitting behind her, having hauled himself awkwardly up to sit gingerly across Moly's loins, put his arms around his wife's slim waist, and thought, And I am the oldest plough horse of all.

Harvest was approaching. The wheat was better than waist-high, and the thatching straw crop was as high as Thwan's shoulder, and Thwan was half a head taller than Pos. It was a good year, and Pos should have been happy, but a shadow had fallen on him, and he could not walk out of it. Coral still rode her mare most afternoons over Buttercup Hill; once he asked her if Moly's shoes still turned gold, and Coral said, after a little pause, that they did. "I had almost forgotten—the noticing and then telling you. It seems as ordinary as—as the sun going behind a cloud, so a great bleak shadow sweeps over you. It's astonishing but at the same time ordinary. It's like that. And it goes away, like that."

But the shadow did not leave Pos, and he began to brood about Buttercup Hill; he thought, angrily, that there was no reason—no proper reason—that a small irregular bit of land should so resist farming. He'd have the weeds down next spring, and cut the ground up well. Ploughing methods had improved since his father's day, and the shape of the blade he used was slightly different. Pos's father and grandfather had probably only not put enough effort into clearing out the buttercup roots; buttercup roots ran everywhere, once they'd had their own way for a few seasons. He and Thwan and Med would dig and plough every last clinging rootlet out, and next year Buttercup Hill would be buttercups no longer.

But simultaneously with this thought was another, about Coral's story. It was nonsense, of course . . . but what if it wasn't? He'd always known that the kind of old tale that gets told around a fireside in the winter, especially late winter when everyone is restless for spring, is a product of nothing more than that restlessness—that and sometimes a need to keep a child quiet. He had known that even when he was the child, something about the tone of his mother's or father's voice; and one or two of those tales had been about Buttercup Hill. He didn't remember them very well; he'd never had children to tell them to, and he had never had much interest in things that weren't true. But the shadow whispered to him, telling him that he had gotten many things wrong in his life and that this was one of them. . . .

He tried to remember the last time he had walked on Buttercup Hill; he wasn't sure he ever had, except for that once, briefly, when his feet touched the bottom of the slope, to keep Coral's arm in his. His father had given up on the problem of its existence years before he was old enough to notice, and he had learned to leave it alone as he had learned to plough and plant and harvest: by doing it. Avoiding it was as ordinary and familiar to him as was the weight of a horse collar in his hand.

One afternoon he arranged to be at that end of the farm when Coral went riding, and he wandered up to the crest of the little hill after her. He thought his feet tingled as he stepped on the buttercups and their hill, and his knees went almost rubbery, but he kept on walking.

The valley was not large, and he saw Moly, Coral bent over her neck, running flat out, graceful as a deer; but the valley came to an end, and she swerved, and Coral drew her up, and in another moment they were trotting up to meet Pos. The whole had taken no more than a few minutes, and Moly had not sweated, though her nostrils showed red as she breathed. "Would you like a try?" said Coral. "Moly has lovely gaits, and a canter is much easier to sit than a trot."

He shook his head, stroking Moly's warm shoulder absently; then he ran his hand down her leg and picked up that hoof. Moly balanced a bit awkwardly, three-legged with a person on her back, and eager as she was for more running; but she was far too well-mannered to protest, and let the hoof lie weightlessly in Pos's big hands. The shoe was yellow—yellow as gold. When Pos touched it, it felt different, not the hard proud absoluteness of cold iron. When he set the foot down and looked up at his wife, she was looking down at him with an expression he had not seen before, and he wondered what the expression on his own face was.

"It's just a shadow over the sun," she said.

"No doubt," he replied.

But two nights later he slipped out to the barn where the horses were kept, leaving Coral asleep. There was a three-quarters moon in a clear sky; the wheat fields were silver.

He drew a long breath; he had been forgetting how much he loved even the smell of his land. It was easy to forget, sometimes, that there was love behind work; it should not be so easy. He was lucky to love his work, and he should make himself remember this if he was so lazy as to forget. He let his eyes wander over the fields, so different from those same fields by daylight. It was going to be a good harvest, better than almost any harvest he could remember. They could afford a new wagon—he and Thwan both were tired of nailing bits back on the old one—and the roof of the lower barn needed replacing, at least the half of it that faced north. His well-organized mind began to make lists, happy in the details of farming, happy in the luck of having been born to work that he loved.

He was luckier yet to have the wife he loved. But the best harvest the farm could produce would not buy her the jewels her beauty deserved, the silks in bright colors she should have to wear, the lofty rooms in the grand house her husband should have been able to offer her. He turned away from the prospect of his moonlit land and went into the barn.

There was a faint sleepy whicker from friendly Moly, who was, Coral had often said, a lapdog grown too large. The big draft horses were silent, knowing the proper schedule, knowing that it was not time for either food or work. Turney came pattering into the barn, having no notion of protecting his territory from invaders but only hoping that the sound of movement might indicate something he could herd. He waved his tail once or twice at Pos in a puzzled fashion and pattered away again.

Pos went into Bel's stall and put a hand on his shoulder; the horse's enormous head came around, but when he saw the bridle in Pos's hand, he flattened his ears and turned his head away again. Pos put his hand over his nose and gently drew him back, feeling the huge neck muscles not quite resisting. Bel was an old horse, well-trained and good-natured too, and he knew it wasn't really worth arguing with human beings. He opened his mouth for the bit with a long sigh.

Pos had chosen Bel because he had the largest feet. He had thought of taking all four workhorses, but decided against it, for reasons he did not quite look at, just as he did not quite look at what he was doing at all.

Pos had to stand on a bucket to scramble up on Bel's broad back; the horse's ears cocked back at this bizarre behavior, but he had made his minor protest in the stall and was now merely bemused. They walked slowly to Buttercup Hill, slowly up it. As Bel's feet first touched the carpet of buttercups, he raised his big head and looked around; Pos briefly had the sensation that he considered prancing. Certainly Pos had not seen him look so interested in anything but his grain bucket in many years.

He turned the horse's head back toward the barn, and as they began the downhill slope, Bel's nose dropped to its usual place, as if he were wearing a collar and pulling a plough. Before they reached the bottom, Pos dismounted and picked one of Bel's feet up. In the moonlight it was difficult to say for sure, for his shoes looked as silvery as the landscape; but under Pos's fingers they tingled, and Pos was sure he saw what he hoped to see. He fumbled for the blacksmith's bar and pincers he had brought with him.

Bel, more bemused than ever, stepped very carefully down the familiar path to the barn, anxious about his naked feet.

Pos slung the heavy satchel of horseshoes down in a corner by the door, and gave Bel a quiet half-portion of grain, to make up for the interruption of his sleep—and Moly a handful of that, since she was awake and lively, putting her nose over her door and trying to seize Pos's sleeve with her lips. She ate the grain happily enough, but she still looked after Pos as if she believed she had been left out of an adventure. The other horses stirred in their drowse, thinking they heard the sound of grain being chewed, but believing they dreamed, for they knew the schedule just as Bel did.

Pos crept back to his sleeping wife, trying to feel pleased with himself and failing; even the moonlight on his beautiful crops did not cheer him, nor the cool rich earth smell in his nostrils. When he eased himself slowly back into bed, Coral turned toward him and murmured, "You're cold. Where have you been?"

"There was a noise in the stock barn," he said, after a moment.

"Moly having adventures in her sleep," said Coral; "you needn't worry, you know, Moly would kick up such a row trying to get any thieves to take notice of her that they'd have little chance to do any mischief. Besides stealing her, I suppose," she added.

"It might have been a bear," said Pos.

"Mmm," said Coral, asleep again.

Pos overslept the next morning, something that had never happened before. It was Coral's cry of shock and terror that awoke him. She was out of bed, standing by the window, and as he sat up, and then stumbled to his feet to go to her, he saw her raise her hands from the windowsill as if she would ward something off, and back away. "The gods have cursed us!" she cried. "What have we done? What have we done? Oh, why did I marry you if it was only to bring you ruin?"

He knew, then, and half expected what he would see when he looked out of the window.

The house and barns stood in a sea of buttercups. Gone were the fields of wheat standing ready for harvest; gone were the neat paths, the fences around the pastures, the smaller tidy blocks of the vegetable garden. He saw a cow blundering unhappily through a tangle of buttercups where the thatching straw had once grown; automatically he recognized her, Flora, always the first one through the gate into fresh pasture, or the first one to find a weak place in the fencing and break through. Behind her at some little distance were Tansy and Nup; the three of them always grazed together, Tansy and Nup following where Flora led. The soft brown and cream of the cows' hair looked dim and weak against the blaze of yellow, as if the cows themselves would be overcome by buttercups, and crumble to pale ash. Pos saw nothing else moving.

Ruined, he thought. More years than are left in my life to regain what I've lost for us both. And he knew that the horseshoes beside the barn door were iron again.

"My darling," said Coral, weeping, "my love, I will go away, back up to the Hills; it is I who caused this. There is a bane on my family, laid on my father's father. He thought to escape it by leaving the mountains, and I thought to escape it by marrying you; almost I did not believe in it, a fey thing, a tale for children, for I was the eldest, and it had not fallen to me, or to Moira after me, but then Del, as he grew up—

no, no, I saw it immediately, when he was just a baby—Moira and I, we both knew, as Rack does, but I *would* not believe, I would make it not so, not for me, it was only a tale, an excuse for recklessness and waste, I believed loving you was enough, that the bane would not follow after a choice honestly made. . . ."

He barely heard her at first, for all he cared about was her distress. He would have to tell her in a moment, tell her that it was he that had ruined them, he and his greed, his dishonest greed, but for the moment he wanted her in his arms, to feel for the last time that his arms were of some use to her, some comfort.

"I could not believe that I was evil, only by having been born into the family that I was; I refused to believe in bad blood, in that kind of wickedness. I believed that you can make what you will of your life; oh, no, I did not really believe that, I did think I was doomed as my family was doomed; till I met you, and fell in love with you, that first day, I think, when I looked up from the well and you were there in that old shabby wagon with your beautiful glossy horse, you were like that yourself, old shabby clothes, but such a good face, and I knew from the way you held the reins that I trusted you—that the horse trusted you—and it was only later that I realized that I loved you. I could not believe my luck when you asked me to marry you; I'm only a girl, and knew nothing of farming, knew nothing of anything except feeding seven people on two potatoes, and horses, I knew horses, I knew that Moly was worth saving when her mother died, although the owner couldn't be bothered.

"Oh, my love," she said, almost incoherent with weeping, "I hate to leave you, but it must have been me; whatever lives in Buttercup Hill recognized me; perhaps if I leave, they

136

will give you your farm back. . . ." She was clinging to him as she never had clung, like ivy on an oak; he had been proud of her independence, that independence choosing to be his companion, to work in his fields with him so that they became their fields; and yet this had been part of what made him uneasy—part of what made him willing to listen to Med. He damned himself now, now that it was too late, for foolishness. He deserved to lose her. But she would not go thinking it was her fault.

"Hush," he said. "It is not your fault. It is not. It is mine. No"—as she began again to speak—"you do not know. I will tell you." But he did not speak at once, and cradled her head against his shoulder in his old knotted hand, and he did not realize that he himself was weeping till he saw the tears fall upon her hair.

"It is I," he said at last, his voice deep with misery, "ah! I hate to tell you. It is true, you must go away, but not to save me, to save yourself." He thought, I can give her a proper dowry if I sell Dor and Thunder; I can get along with Bel and Ark only, for I will have to let Med and Thwan go, of course. With her beauty she will be able to find another husband; and with some money she will be able to find one who will respect her. . . .

"Tell me," she said, and drew her head away, and looked up at him. "Tell me," she said, passionately.

"I cannot, if you look at me like that," he said, closing his eyes, and now he felt the hot tears on his cheeks. He felt her move, and her hands on his face, and her lips against his chin. "I love you," she said. "I am *glad*"—she said fiercely—"if this is not my fault, for then I need not leave you after all."

That gave him the strength to tell her, and as he had told

her nothing before, he told her all now, for he could not decide what to tell and what to hold back. So he began with Med, and of how Med's words had made him look at what he had turned away from before, that he was an old man, too old for her, and dull, a farmer, with little enough to offer her, except that her own family—here, finally, he stumbled over his words—had so much less. And he thought that perhaps if he had money enough to buy her things—the sorts of things beautiful women should have—perhaps that would be enough, that she would find it enough reason to stay with him. . . . He stopped himself just before he told her he could not bear to lose her, because he was going to send her away, for he had nothing at all to offer her now.

She was silent for a time after he had spoken, but she did not draw away as he expected. Her hands had gone around his neck while he spoke, and her head was again in the curve between his collarbone and jaw. At last she sighed and stepped back, and he dropped his hands instantly, but she just as quickly took them in her own, and looked into his face with her clear eyes and smiled. "It is very bad," she said, "but not so bad as I expected—feared. For I do not have to leave you after all. I wish—I wish we had talked of this six months ago, for you are an escape for me, and I have never not known this, nor ignored that you are my father's age. But I was too afraid to tell you everything about me—and you have known that I did not tell you everything, and that is how this began.

"No," she said, as he would have spoken. "No. I will not listen, for I know now what you would say, and I will not have it. We are both at fault, and we will work together to mend that fault; and after this we will tell each other—not everything, for who can tell everything even if they wished?

Who can tell everything, even to oneself? Not I. But I have known there were important things I was not telling you, and we will make a vow, now, to tell each other everything we know to be important. And"—she laughed, a little, a poor sound compared with her usual laughter, but a laugh nonetheless—"and we will trust our own judgment about importance, for we have had a very hard lesson."

She clasped their hands together tightly and said, "Promise. Promise me now, as I promise you, to tell you—tell you as much of everything as I can, and I will look into all the shadows that I can for things that need to be told, and perhaps I will even learn to ask you to help me to look for shadows. And there will be no shame between us about this, about what is important, about what shadows we fear—about those very things we most fear to tell each other. Promise." And she shook their clasped hands.

"Coral—"

"*Promise.*"

And so he promised.

And then they went downstairs together, and ate a hasty breakfast, and went out to see what could be done, and to decide where to start.

Med went willingly. Pos, looking into his eyes before Med dropped his, saw something there that made him—for all the disaster around him—glad for the excuse to let him go, never having had any notion before this that such an excuse was wanted.

But Thwan would not leave. "I've known about Buttercup Hill," he said, easily giving it the friendly name Coral had used in better times. "My father's father told stories of it too, Pos. It's a danger we live by, like a river that may flood. I can afford to work for no wages for a little while. I don't want much but work to do." He paused, but Pos was thinking of likening Buttercup Hill to a river. Rivers did not only destroy, when they ran beyond their banks. Thwan went on, slowly: "Good work to do. And I'm too old to be finding another master. Even if one would have me, I'm used to doing things . . . the way of this farm." He paused again. "I don't think what lives in Buttercup Hill means you to starve, and starving is the only thing that frightens me."

Pos looked at his old friend half in dismay and half in delight. He had not told him why the buttercups had flooded the farm; only Coral need know that. He would find something for Thwan to do at the other end of the farm while he hammered Bel's shoes back on; Thwan would not ask for an explanation, but Pos would know he was not offering one. That easily he accepted Thwan's refusal. He had not, then, the strength to argue, there was too much else his strength was needed for more; but while he did not know it, losing that first argument with Coral had turned him to a new shape. The littleness of the change was such that it would be a long time before he knew of it. But what it meant, now, was that he could let his wife and his farmhand overrule his decision and he lose no face or authority and gain no shame from it. He did not think of this at all. He thought of starving, and of the buttercups where the vegetable garden had been; of whether cows could give milk when their only forage was buttercups. And so Thwan stayed.

And they did not starve, the three of them, because for the first deadly hard weeks Coral went out in the mornings with panniers behind Moly's saddle into the wild land beyond the farm, and gathered berries and other fruit, and dug roots and cut succulent young leaves, and brought them home, for she had had long years of feeding a larger family on almost nothing. She refused to accept any praise for this; it was harvest time in the wild too, and there was plenty to eat, and no cleverness necessary in the gathering of it. She taught Pos, who had never known, and Thwan, who had forgotten, how to set snares; and they ate rabbit and hare and ootag. Sometimes Thwan ate with them in the evenings, which he had not done before; it seemed easier, that way, to share equally, when there was only just enough. The noon meal was as it had always been, something on the back of the stove, set there to cook when Pos, and later Pos and Coral, came outdoors in the morning; except on the hottest days, when it was bread and cheese. But previously the noon meal had been eaten out of doors, under a tree, on the porch, in a corner of a field; and all three of them noticed that Thwan was now the only one who seemed still to prefer this. Both Pos and Coral spoke to him about it, but he only smiled, and they saw in the smile that he did not stay away from the house from shyness.

But for worry, they were all as healthy and strong as they had ever been.

Strength they needed, and stamina. The first thing they did was look out the fencing for the animals, and it was not as bad as they had expected, for the fencing was still there, under the wild weave of buttercups. It was only that—mysteriously—all the gates had been opened on the night that Pos had pulled Bel's shoes off after walking on Buttercup Hill.

More mysteriously, the beasts all ate buttercups with apparent relish. (Even Turney, who did not know that his three human beings were careful to leave something on their plates for the dog's bowl when they would have liked to eat the last scrap themselves, was seen gravely nipping the heads off buttercups, and swallowing them enthusiastically.) The cows' milk had never been so thick and rich and abundant as in the first buttercup weeks, for all that their calves were half grown and they should be beginning to dry up toward winter. Even the sheep's udders swelled, though this was at first unnoticed since unexpected, invisible under their thick curling fleeces (thicker than usual, thought Pos; must be coming up a bad winter). The horses seemed tireless, however many times they went up and down the fields pulling Pos's heaviest blade, for the buttercup roots went deep (a rare crop of poppies we'll have next year, thought Pos).

"In case you'd like to know," said Coral, "this proves that they aren't buttercups. Real buttercups are poisonous." (Slow-acting, thought Pos. Cumulative. The stock will all die suddenly, any time now.)

Pos taught Coral to make cheese, and after they'd had a few weeks to ripen, risked taking a few cheeses they hoped were surplus to market day in town; and these fetched prices better than their previous cheeses ever had, after Coral brought enough over from their lunch the first time to offer small sample tastes (wasteful, thought Pos). And then the three cows that had been barren in the spring dropped unsuspected calves at the very end of summer, and the calves were bigger and stronger than any Pos had seen in all his years of farming, although the mothers had found the births easy. These calves grew so quickly that Coral said to Pos that she felt that if she ever had time to stand still for a quarter hour and watch, she would see them expand. "We could ask Thwan to eat his lunch next to the cow pasture," she suggested with a grin, "and ask if he sees anything."

Pos shook his head. "Something not right about them,"

he said. "Something grows too quickly in the beginning, gets spindly before the end, doesn't grow together right."

When Pos took all the calves to the big harvest fair in late autumn, the youngest ones were almost as well-grown as the oldest. It was one of the youngest that fetched the best price of all, and the farmer who bought her exclaimed over the heavy straight bones and clean lines of her, how square and sturdy she was built.

Several people remarked on the slight golden cast of the coats and hoofs and eyes of those last three calves, just as other people remarked that they could pick out one of Buttercup Farm's new cheeses because it glowed as it lay among other, more ordinary fare, just as their sheep's wool, which had only looked like any wool on the sheep's backs, proved to have a faint golden tint when it was washed and spun.

Winter was a lean time nonetheless, for they had had little harvest. The wheat and straw crops were ruined, though there were vegetables left under the buttercup vines as there had been fence posts and rails under them, and so they did not starve; but they had none left over to sell, and before spring they began to wish they had sold fewer cheeses, though they had spent every penny they earned on stores for the winter, for the beasts as well as themselves, and for seed for the spring. There was nothing over even to mend the old wagon, which was at its creakiest and most fragile in cold weather.

It was a hard winter (though not as hard as Pos predicted). Snow fell, and no one had any good winter crops, and what little grew was tough and dry and frostbitten. But when the spring came and the horses drew the plough through the fresh-cut furrows one last time before setting seed, the plough seemed to fly through the earth, although its blade glinted gold rather than silver, and Bel's and Ark's flaxen manes were almost yellow. And the buttercups still twined over all the fencing, even the stair rails up to the porch around the house, and showed flowers early, as soon as the snow melted, before most other leaves were even thinking about putting in an appearance. (Pos said that the buttercups hid mending that needed to be done, and that Flora would be finding the weak places for them.)

The cows all delivered their calves safely, and none was barren, and the sheep delivered their lambs, which were mostly twins, but the grass rose up thickly enough to support any amount of milk for any number of babies, and cheese-making besides. The cheeses this year were as yellow as they had been the autumn before, and the new babies again touched with gold; and then bright chestnut Moly threw a foal, though she had not been bred that they knew, and the farm horses were all mares and geldings. The foal was as golden as a new penny, and as fleet as a bird, with legs even longer than its dam's as it grew up, and they called it Feyling, and when it was four years old, Coral rode it at the harvest fair races, and it won the gold cup.

But by then Coral was pregnant with their second child, and Merry was two and a half, and Pos had not wanted Coral to ride in the race, but she had only laughed and said that she was glad she was no more than three months along, for she did not want to weigh enough to slow Feyling down. "Not that anything could," she added, and Pos knew that there was no point in arguing with her.

Their farm had been called Buttercup Farm from that first grim but surprising autumn, and while they had taken no joy from the name initially, they let it stand, not wishing to disturb what it was they had involuntarily set in motion, or set free, or roused, whatever it was that, as Thwan had said, did not in fact wish them to starve, and when anyone asked if they were from Buttercup Farm, they said with only a momentary pause, "Yes." The momentary pause had disappeared by the time the year had come around to harvest again, and Thwan had come to Pos, much embarrassed, and said that he wished to marry too, and Pos had said with real feeling that he did not wish to lose him but would try to put together the money he was certainly owed, that they might make a beginning toward their own farm. And Thwan said, after a pause, in his slow way, that all they really wanted was enough to build a little house, on the edge of Buttercup Farm, if Pos and Coral would allow it, and he go on working as he had done for so long, and perhaps there would be work for his wife too; she was raised on a farm. They had met over Buttercup Farm cheeses, because people had begun to come in from the next counties to buy them, and she knew something about cheeses.

A year after Thwan married Nai, they increased their cow and sheep herds by almost a half, to keep up with the demand for their cheeses; but there they stopped it, for they were happy with their work, and the size of their farm, and each other, and they tried not to make too many plans for Merry, and for Thwan and Nai's Orly, and for the baby Coral was carrying when Feyling won the gold cup. But when they built the house for Thwan to bring Nai home to, they shook buttercup pollen over it, and the vines obligingly grew up their porch railings the next year too, but politely left room for Nai's pansies. And when Pos and Coral repainted their house, white as it had always been, they stripped the black shutters down to bare wood so they could repaint them a pale yellow, as they painted the railings around the porch the same color, and it gleamed against the darker buttercups. They had never had time, that first year, to uproot the vines that grew around their house, although Pos at least had wished to; but neither of them now would think of it (although Coral took cuttings from Nai, and planted pansies), and the vines just around the house went on bearing flowers nine or ten months of the year, an occasional yellow spangle showing even when all else was dry and brown and cold.

After Feyling won the gold cup, he was much in demand at stud, though no one knew who his father was, and no one was greedy or stupid enough to claim a stolen stud fee. And Pos learned to ride, first on the good-natured Moly and later on the less patient Feyling, and so Coral took her husband with her now on her afternoon rides, when there was time and peace for them again. But they did not ride on Buttercup Hill.

After Dhwa was born, and that spring was more glorious even than the last four springtimes had been, the four of them, Pos and Coral and Merry and Dhwa went, one night under a full moon, to walk on Buttercup Hill. They had not set foot there since Bel had walked shoeless over it; but over the years they no longer felt a chill as they passed it, and began to seek it out with their eyes, and feel as if it were a friendly presence, and to be pleased when their work took them near it.

They walked up to the little crest, Dhwa in Coral's arms and Merry set down to toddle around her father's feet, the children's hair no less yellow than the untouched tangle of buttercups in the hollow before them, golden even in the moonlight. There was a tiny breeze, and a wonderful smell of green growing things, and a distant whiff of clean barn and animals and their fodder. Pos and Coral gave long sighs, and leaned against each other, carefully, for Dhwa was asleep. Pos it was who at last spoke aloud what they were both thinking.

"Thank you," he said.

A *K*not
in the Grain

*T*hey moved upstate ten days after the end of school, a week after her sixteenth birthday. It had been the worst party of her life, because it was supposed to be a birthday party, but it was really a farewell party, and all the presents were good-byes. The music was as loud as ever, and everybody danced and shouted and ate chips and cookies the way they always did. She and Bridget ate most of the carrot and red- and green-pepper sticks to make her mother happy. Annabelle's mom insisted there be good-for-you munchies at her daughter's parties, but Bridget was usually on a diet and really appreciated them, and Annabelle had developed a taste for pepper sticks on potato chips, like a kind of misguided taco. But nothing tasted good that night. It wasn't the same and everybody knew it. Polly burst into tears when she left, and then all the girls started crying, and the boys stood around looking awkward and patting their girls' shoulders in that way boys have when they want to look as if they're being sympathetic but what they really want is for you to stop whatever it is you're doing, like crying, or having a serious conversation. She'd both cried and tried to have serious conversations with Bill several times in the last weeks.

Bill stuck around after everyone else had left, in spite of the probability of more tears. He helped her clean up and stack dishes in the dishwasher, and that he also ate the last four brownies without asking, assuming that it was part of the deal that if he helped with the work, he could do pretty much whatever else he liked, was just Bill. She knew he was a good guy basically, and that he liked her. She knew that he didn't just like her because her parents let her have parties in their big living room with any kind of music they wanted, and never objected to how much they ate.

She didn't herself understand why she couldn't appreciate it more that he was a good guy. He never teased her about certain things that her girlfriends seemed to think boys always teased you about. Like having sex with him. (A nasty little voice in her mind had once suggested to her that that would have given her an excuse to break up with him. But she didn't want that kind of excuse. Did she?) Or having beer at her parties, which her parents wouldn't allow, although if one or two friends were over for supper with the family, they were offered a glass of beer or wine. He liked that. He liked it so much that they'd had to talk about it. What was there to talk about? Rules were rules, and parents sometimes knew what they were talking about. She wasn't sorry not to have alcohol at her parties because some of the kids who wouldn't come because of that were the ones she didn't want to come anyway. But Bill had really gotten into what he called the difference between freedom and responsibility, and she'd seen him suddenly at about forty-five, with a bald spot and a second chin, still going on about rules.

She'd known Bill since fifth grade, and they would have

been going together for a year in August—except she wouldn't be here in August. And she knew that if she hadn't had the excuse that they were moving, she would have had to find some other reason to break up with him. It was the only even marginally okay thing about their moving. So she watched Bill eating the last brownies and decided not to say anything. Her head felt heavy and swollen with unshed tears; it was as if the tear reservoir had opened, but then some of the tears were dammed up again by an unexpected sluice gate partway downstream, the sluice gate of Bill's discomfort. She felt sloshy and stupid, as if her brain were soggy, squelching like a wrung sponge under the pressure of thinking.

By this August Susan would probably have got Bill, and then he and Susan would write her these half-phony, half-sincere apologetic letters about how they hoped she didn't mind too much. It might be Milly, who wouldn't feel she owed Annabelle any letters, but Annabelle was betting on Susan.

The things you found yourself thinking at one o'clock in the morning after the last party you were ever going to have with all your friends. She came back to herself with a tea-towel in her hand, drying off her mother's blue glass bowl, which wouldn't fit in the dishwasher. Bill was smiling at her fondly; he thought he knew what she was thinking, and he was almost right. Her eyes filled with tears involuntarily, and he put his arms around her (after taking the bowl away from her and carefully setting it down on the counter) and said, "There, there," without any implication that he would rather she didn't. She was so grateful she didn't cry after all, but snuffled violently for a minute, choking the tears back down again. And so in the end she kissed Bill quietly good-bye, and watched him walking down the sidewalk till he disappeared under the trees.

She thought about her birthday party again the day the movers came. The living room was full of cardboard boxes, which had been stacked in the hall for the party. Most of her friends came around at some point that day to say good-bye again, more officially, more briefly, more helplessly. There really wasn't anything left to say except "good-bye," and "I'll miss you," and "I'll write." A few of them would write: Bill, for example, faithfully, till August and Susan. She'd know when he skipped a week for the first time. She told herself she didn't care. She didn't—not about Bill; but she cared about herself, and she was lonesome. She was already lonely without all her friends, and they hadn't even left yet.

Her parents were impatient to be gone, so they closed up the house Annabelle had lived in for fourteen years at five o'clock that afternoon, as soon as the movers had gone, and drove out of town. Annabelle tried not to turn and look down her old street for the last time, but at the last she failed, whirling around just before they reached the corner, staring at the double row of maples lining the street and the enormous oak tree in their front yard, the first tree she'd ever climbed, and the first tree she'd ever fallen out of. They caught up with the movers' truck shortly after they reached the highway.

They ate supper at a highway-side fast-food restaurant, so Annabelle didn't miss much by having no appetite. And they arrived at their new home a few minutes before midnight, and all three of them were almost too tired to stagger up the steep walk, find bedrooms, unpack sheets and toothbrushes, and fall into proper beds, instead of staying slumped in the car. "You're right, Annabelle," said her father, although she hadn't said anything; "it would have been easier to stay in a motel." Annabelle was too tired to smile.

She knew where she was before she woke up; it was as if some portion of her mind had stayed guard while the rest of her slept, and it warned her that she was no longer at home, or in any of the semi-familiar other beds she had occasionally woken up in: in her grandmother's spare room, or Uncle Tim and Aunt Rita's, or the other bed in Bridget's room or Polly's. This was a strange bed in a strange room in a strange place. She opened her eyes.

After they'd bought the house last summer, knowing that Dad was retiring and they would move up here this summer, they'd bought a few things for the extra rooms that their old house didn't have, her mother, in her usual sensible way, pointing out that this would make moving in much easier as well, since the movers would (in the mysterious way of movers) take two days to cover the same miles it took the family six hours to travel. And then there would be the days and weeks of unpacking, and the absolutely vital boxes that would have gone missing. . . . You'd think Mom had spent most of her life moving house, Annabelle had said to Polly. "Nah," said Polly. "It's just that once you've been an executive secretary your mind can't stop thinking that way."

Annabelle had tried to be grateful for the two extra years she knew she'd had in her old town: two years for Mom to get her quilting business set up so she could run it by mail, two years that Dad had spent teaching only half time so he could spend the other half doing research for two or three of the six or ten books he wanted to get written. (He had gotten three written while teaching full-time, while Annabelle was growing up; it was just the sound of Saturday and Sunday mornings, Dad's typewriter going in the study off the kitchen, when Annabelle came downstairs for weekend breakfasts after as late a night as she could keep her eyes open for, reading or watching TV or later going to quadruple features at the mall cinema.) But he said the really interesting books wouldn't come while half his mind was still preoccupied with students. Annabelle couldn't tell if his books were interesting or not; they all began with self-deprecating introductions that only other Ph.D.'s in American intellectual history could understand, and went on from there.

Annabelle had liked having a mother who wasn't an executive secretary any more; it had always taken her an hour or two in the evenings to turn back into Mom from a kind of sharp-edged walking Filofax that told you a little too briskly that the table needed to be laid and why hadn't the floor gotten vacuumed as promised? (She got after Dad in the same voice she got after Annabelle, so it wasn't too bad.) But Annabelle also knew what the mounting piles of swatches and order forms spilling out of the little room under the stairs and taking over one end of the dining room table meant: They meant that her mother was making a success of putting her mail-order soft toys and quilts and silly-cloth-portraiture business together. (It was the ad that had the photo of the portrait she'd done of the president that really got the thing going; there were more people out there with a sense of humor about their government than Annabelle would have expected or, really, entirely, approved of. If the president was the pits, why did they elect him?)

She'd known that privately Mom and Dad had agreed

they would give themselves up to three years, although they hoped to do it in two. They'd started house-hunting two years ago—farther and farther south and inland, in smaller and smaller towns, as they discovered the facts about what their savings would buy—because two years was the official number in the family. The family was Mom and Dad and Annabelle, and also Averil and Ted and Sylvia, all of them married now and Averil and Sylvia with kids of their own. Sylvia had warned Annabelle that Mom did what she set out to and that if she said two years and not three, it was going to be two years. Annabelle didn't need the warning; it was the sort of thing Sylvia did, telling people, especially her little sister, stuff they already knew.

But Annabelle hadn't been able not to hope, at least a little, secretly, because if it had been three years, surely they wouldn't have made her leave and go to a new school for just her senior year? That would have been cruel. Rationally she knew that that was a significant part of why Mom said two years: so that Annabelle would have two years in a new school. But Annabelle had been surprised at how strong that small private hope had gotten, squeezed away in its dark corner, when she'd had to give it up.

Annabelle sat up cautiously in the unfamiliar bed in the unfamiliar room and looked out the unfamiliar window. She was opposite the one dormer window in a long narrow attic room; when she'd chosen this room last summer as where she'd spend her first few nights, until her bed and bedroom gear arrived and she could unpack into her real bedroom downstairs, her mother had protested: "You'll just scare yourself up there, in a big old empty strange house. I'm not going to stand around and let you set yourself up to dislike it here."

"I'm not," said Annabelle. "I'll be okay. I like the view." Her mother, not convinced, but not wanting to make too many issues of things when she knew how Annabelle felt about having to move at all, let it go.

Annabelle knew that her mother was not entirely wrong about her choosing the attic perversely, deliberately accentuating her feeling of alienation about the whole business of the move; but it was also true that she did like the view, and the flicker of weak pleasure it gave her was about the only pleasure she'd felt about any of it so far. Her bedroom downstairs faced the same direction, but the extra two floors of height made it much more dramatic.

The house had been built originally by one of the smallish local railroad barons, who, with his railroad, had shortly thereafter gone bust; and the house had been bought by an enterprising farmer who had planted an orchard behind it, built on a long two-storey wing for his increasing family, and grown hay and wheat and corn in the fields beyond, some of which were now meadow and some of which were now streets with newer, smaller houses on them. But this house had stood empty for most of the last fifteen years; it had been rented out in the summers occasionally while the heirs quarrelled over the terms of the will; but while they were quarrelling, they were not willing to fix the roof or put in modern plumbing, and so none of this had been done till even summer visitors had balked. Annabelle's family, four months after the remaining heirs had come to terms, bought the house and ten acres for, as her father put it, a song. "Not even a song. A sort of warm-up exercise, like Czerny before you tackle the Beethoven sonata."

"The Beethoven sonata is what it'll cost us to fix it up,"

Mom had replied, half grimly and half with that lilt of *challenge* in her voice that her family knew well.

"Yup," said Dad, not the least repentant. They both liked challenges.

"Why else would they have had the four of us?" said Ted, the one with no children. Ted was the easy-going one, surrounded by people who liked challenges, including his wife, Rebecca, who was a social worker specializing in schizophrenic adolescents and reform school escapees. Annabelle thought, clutching the bedclothes to her chin, that maybe she was more like Ted than the rest of the family.

But the view was terrific. A lot of the orchard was still there, but the trees were set well apart, and Annabelle was high enough up, in the peak of the oldest part of the house, to look straight over their heads besides. There was a long low grassy meadow slope to the river, which she could see even at this distance twinkle and flash with speed in the sunlight. It was a beautiful day. The movers wouldn't get here till tomorrow afternoon, and Annabelle thought probably her parents would let her alone today so long as she didn't let herself be seen hanging around moping. She'd get up, have breakfast, and wander—no, walk purposefully—down to the river.

Her mother was already cleaning cupboards, the air harsh with the smell of Pine Sol and Comet. Annabelle picked up two Dunkin' Donuts from the box on the kitchen table (her father would have made a point of finding the nearest Dunkin' Donuts before he signed the papers on the house) and went out through the back door onto the porch. Across one end there was a dusty old canvas hammock with a fringe.

159

She sat on it gingerly, listening to the old ropes creak, and ate a doughnut which tasted slightly of canvas dust. "What are you doing?" said her mother, her head suddenly emerging from a window.

"Going down to the river," Annabelle said, instantly jumping to her feet and starting down the porch steps.

"Don't get lost," said her mother in a milder tone, and Annabelle waved a sugary hand.

She ate the other doughnut on the way and then washed her hands in the quick cold water. The river—more of a wide brook—was shallow here, with green weed streaming along its bottom: trout, she thought. She'd find someone to ask if there were fish in the river, and if so, if you could eat them.

Now that she was out of easy recall distance of the house she no longer had to walk purposefully, and she ambled, looking at the reeds on the riverbank, and watching small brown birds she couldn't name hustle through the undergrowth, and others dart through the trees farther up the bank. There was a sort-of path which she followed, going uphill till it became quite steep; and then there began to be the backs of people's lawns, mown down to the river, and the sort-of path became gravel and then tar, and ended at a low brick wall. On the other side were a road, and the kind of little shops that a year-round village with heavy summer tourist trade had on its main street.

She turned left at random, toward what looked like the center of town: an unsquare square with grass and small, relentlessly tidy beds of pansies and petunias around a statue of some local worthy on a horse. The town hall was on the far side, and the town library was beyond it. Annabelle could always recognize a library.

She wouldn't be able to get a library card yet; she'd need

her parents, or an envelope that had obviously been through the post office that had her name and new address on it, or both, or something else. But she could ask. Maybe they'd give her an application to take home. And it would give her the excuse to look the library over. If it was a good library, that would be two and a half things about the move that were okay. (Was it Bill or the view from the attic that was the half? Bill, she decided, after a moment's thought, but it might have been guilt that made the decision.)

They gave her the application and pointed, with some pride, toward the new wing, and did not merely offer but encouraged her to go look. "The children's and young adults' room was just finished this spring," the lady who'd handed her the application said.

It was too big and too glossy; the doorway was huge, and she felt, walking through it, that a laser beam would skewer her and a voice out of "Star Trek" would ask her what she was doing there and that her answer wouldn't be good enough. But there were reassuringly full shelves once she got through. The picture books were segregated, grouped to make a little room within a room around tiny plastic chairs and tables in bright primary colors; the rest of the books were in a delicious muddle, from *The Reluctant Dragon*, which Mom had first read her when she was not quite four, to *The Last Unicorn*, which she'd read herself out of the adult science fiction a couple of years ago in her old library. She browsed along, backing up and jumping forward through the alphabet, as she thought of authors she wanted to look for. She was following the D's around a corner when she came abruptly to the end of the bunched shelving, and found herself walking into a big empty space, sunlit both from the sides and overhead, and with big low ugly chairs of the well-meaning public

161

rec room variety sold to town councils with more spirit than money. There were half a dozen kids of about her age sitting there: four girls and two boys. She stopped as if she'd walked into a wall.

They stared at one another for a moment; or they stared at her, and she stared at the fact of them without being able to take in much about any of them. After a few long seconds one of the girls smiled slightly; Annabelle saw the smile but couldn't tell if it was friendly or scornful. "Hi," she made herself say. "Hi," said the girl who'd smiled, but she didn't say anything else, and the others said nothing at all. Annabelle realized she was clutching the application form painfully against her stomach. She turned away and, trying not to look as if she were fleeing, left the library.

The movers arrived earlier the next day than anticipated, and then serious chaos began. Annabelle helped sweep and scrub and restack boxes and unpack and put away—and then put away somewhere else—without too much grumbling. She didn't have anything better to do, and she didn't mind physical labor. The third okay thing about the move was that they were going to have a proper garden here, room for vegetables and flowers, and she could do some of the digging and weeding.

She took the library application back and got her library card, and the library really was okay, she just stayed away from the rec room chairs at the end of the young adults' room and went around the shelves at the other end. She explored the adult section too, which was older and grimier and not as well lit, and didn't have any chairs at all, so if you wanted to try a paragraph or a page of something, you had to sit on a step-stool or the floor.

About a week after the movers had come, she let herself notice that she was still sleeping in the attic. Or rather her mother noticed for her. "I like it up there," she said. "I like the view."

"You said that before," said her mother. "It's still low and dark and far away from the rest of the house—I mean the part we're living in; it'll take a while to reclaim all of it."

"And then we'll open a bed and breakfast," said Dad from behind his book.

"Um," said Mom, who preferred to tackle her challenges one at a time. "I'm not sure I like you that far away. The view's the same one you have from downstairs."

"Not really," said Annabelle. "Come up and see."

So her mother did, and saw what Annabelle meant, but wasn't going to give in yet. "Maybe when we're a little more unpacked and moved in," said Mom. "Maybe when it's not such a disaster area downstairs."

Annabelle knew she was feeling guilty. The room she was going to use for her office and workroom had turned out to be infested with something or other, and the smell of the stuff the exterminator had used really hung around, so its door was closed and its windows were open, and meanwhile Mom was using all of the dining room, not just the end of the table, and it really was a disaster area. Not to mention that the stinky room was next to what was supposed to be Annabelle's bedroom. Although it really didn't smell in Annabelle's bedroom, or even the hall outside.

"Maybe," said Annabelle. And they left it at that.

Annabelle spent a lot of her time reading, upstairs in her attic. She reread all of E. Nesbit, Edward Eager, L. Frank Baum, Eleanor Farjeon, from the library, feeling a little bemused by the strange copies of her old friends, in their plastic protectors, someone else's fingerprints on the pages. Hers were still lying in a box downstairs somewhere, and dusty with several years' neglect. She'd gotten on the junior high yearbook staff in seventh grade—rather a feather in her cap, you didn't usually get picked till eighth—and from then on she'd had less time for reading, and told herself she was outgrowing the fantasy and fairy tales that had been her favorite escape through childhood. When she got into high school and started taking advanced English courses, she kept herself busy with stuff on reading lists; she'd read *War and Peace* for extra credit over the summer last year, and the rest of the time had been taken up with Bridget and Poll and Bill and the rest of them. She told herself she didn't need books about imaginary places and things that weren't real. But she knew she wouldn't have had to go on telling herself this if it were really true. So another sort of okay thing about the move became that she let herself read anything she wanted, and didn't even look at the "classics for young adults" reading list hanging on a chain by the librarians' desk. But it was a little scary, too, because she knew she was older, and wondered if she was going backward somehow, and the stories sometimes looked different from what she remembered, and some she liked better than she had and some worse.

Bill wrote her every five days or so, just as she'd expected, bland good-guy letters studded with unconscious arrogance, just like Bill in person. She answered faithfully, talking about the house and the river and the town; she didn't mention that she was reading fairy tales, and she didn't mention that she didn't have anyone to talk to except Mom and Dad, although she closed each letter by saying that she missed him. It was true, in a way. She missed having friends.

When Bridget's first letter came and she saw her old friend's big sprawly handwriting across the envelope—handwriting that looked almost the same as it had in third grade, when they first learned cursive—she'd burst into tears, amazing herself and distressing her parents. "Oh, honey—" said her mother, putting her arm around Annabelle's shoulders.

"It's okay, it's okay," sobbed Annabelle, and went upstairs to her attic again.

She didn't read the letter till the next day. Bridget sounded just like Bridget, too, even more than Bill sounded like Bill, although that might just be because she found Bridget more interesting. It took her a long time, because her eyes kept filling up, reading the ten pages of Bridget's letter: what would be three or four in anyone else's writing, and with fewer exclamation points and dashes. Between paragraphs Annabelle looked up and sniffed, staring mostly out across what she now thought of as her view down to the river; but occasionally she looked down the length of the attic, admiring the way the heavy beams met in the center, the smoothness of the laid boards; there was something about the organization of it (perhaps she was her mother's daughter after all), about the deliberate purposefulness of the roof of a house, this house, now her house. This purposefulness was comforting in a way that the river view wasn't; the charm of the long grass and the water was the motion of it; the comfort of the shape of the roof, the straight lines and angles of it, was that it was motionless.

The new people had moved into their old house, Bridget wrote, and they had three little kids; the bunk beds in the attic that Annabelle's dad had put in for the teenage Averil and Ted must be in use again. And they'd put up a new swing from the same branch of the oak tree that Annabelle's old swing had hung from; and they'd asked Bridget to baby-sit, but she couldn't bear to, she thought, though she was curious to know what the inside of the house looked like now. . . .

Annabelle got up from the pile of mismatched pillows that made her two-dollar armchair comfortable (the same flea market where they'd bought the white-painted iron bedstead for fifteen dollars, last summer), and went to rub her hand down the beam nearest her. It was a little darker than the one matching it on the other side of the peak, and there was a big knot in it, and knots were often particularly lovely under the fingertips.

She was concentrating on the feel of the knot, her eyes half closed and not attending; but it's when you're not thinking about noticing, and therefore don't have it in your mind what you expect to see, that you're likeliest to see something unexpected. And Annabelle saw a long thin straight crack in the beam, meeting another long thin straight crack in the beam at a right angle. . . . She dropped her hand, widened her eyes. . . . Hinges, looking like thin blackened splinters of wood. Now she raised both hands and began to feel along the cracks. . . . Hook. Just a simple flat black iron hook in a tiny bulge of eye. No, two of them. She might have slept and read and worked and mooned around in this attic for years without noticing if it hadn't been for the misery-inspired desire to rub her fingers across that knot.

She pulled the hooks free. Nothing happened. Her fingers investigated again, looking for something to pull on. Still nothing. She could get no purchase on the hooks themselves. Letter opener on her bureau. She slid it into the crack and jiggled, ran it the length of the crack, down its two sides, and then back to the should-be-freed crack opposite the hinges. Wiggle. Wiggle. *Wiggle.*

A faint creak, like the sorts of ghostly noises old houses are supposed to make; but it was bright sunshine, and for the first time in weeks Annabelle was too occupied to be lonely. And with the creak, the two edges slipped apart, just a little—but enough for Annabelle to get her fingers against the freshly revealed margin and pull till her joints hurt. It gave a little more; her fingers crept up the edge again, and this time the width of the door or wall or whatever it was came free, and she could hook her fingers over it (into the blackness on the other side—she wouldn't think about that) and pull properly. More creaking noises, rather louder now. Annabelle tugged and tugged, in little jerks, then more positive ones, trying to use the full weight of her body against the stubbornness of an ancient, stuck-shut hidey-hole; then in little jerks again as she tired. Leverage, she thought, and went out to the landing halfway down the attic stairs, where she had left a broom and a dustpan, and brought the broom back. Stuffed the broom handle in the opening, leaned on it—and the broom handle broke.

"Hell," said Annabelle, and stopped, letting her excitement cool enough for her to think about the situation. Crowbar, she thought. There was a crowbar at home—she still thought of the old house in her old town that way when she was talking only to herself, but she was careful not to say it aloud in her parents' hearing—in the garage; would it have been unpacked yet? Only one way to find out.

She didn't see it, but she got the tire iron out of the back of the car instead, hoping her parents wouldn't see her and ask what she was doing; it was mysteriously desirable for her to solve this puzzle, make this discovery by herself. No one saw her. The tire iron wasn't ideally shaped, but at least she couldn't break it, and the old wood of the house was granite-hard, and the iron's pressure left no mark.

She got it open about a hand's breadth by lunchtime. She'd lost track of time, and her mother had come halfway up the stairs to call her. Annabelle rushed out to stop her coming the rest of the way, and then stopped herself just out of sight, for she was too dusty and dishevelled (and a bit greasy from the things the tire iron picked up at the bottom of the trunk of the car) not to arouse comment. "I'm sorry. I'm just coming. Go ahead without me."

Her mother's steps retreated, and Annabelle flew down to the bathroom to scrub off and comb her hair. "There's another reason to get you out of that attic," her mother said, half teasing and half glad of any other reason, however minor and domestic. "It's too far to walk when you don't hear me the first time."

"We can get an intercom," said Annabelle. "I'm sorry. I do usually hear."

She went back upstairs immediately after lunch, despite her mother's trying to persuade her to go outdoors: Mom always thought sunlight was good for you—working in sunlight, that is. Lying on a beach blanket was bad for you, nothing to do with holes in the ozone and skin cancer. But at the moment she *had* to go back to the attic and the wider— widening—black crack in the low-pitched roof. She quietly raided the pantry on her way, for a flashlight and candles, visible among half-unpacked boxes.

It took her most of another hour to get it open—open enough. It was a set of stairs, very narrow but steep, built against the other side of the ceiling, and probably supposed to rest on the floor when fully open. She got them down to about six inches of the floor and gave up; the huge black space revealed was plenty big enough for her to walk up . . . a much less attractive prospect now than the first impulse to find out what the hinged crack was about had suggested. She'd supposed there would be a secret cupboard, something she could comfortably see into from the sunlit attic; or rather she hadn't thought very clearly about it at all, just that this was an adventure, and an adventure might be fun. She looked back to Bridget's letter, still lying where she'd left it on the floor next to the armchair by the window. Flea market furniture had its virtues; you didn't feel obliged to worry about the sun fading it. She looked out at the bright afternoon and thought about the sun on her back as she stooped in their garden-to-be. Then she picked up the flashlight and turned it on. She put candles and matches in her pockets, and started up the steps.

The stairs made horrible noises, even more horrible than when she'd tried jumping on the bottom stair to try to open them fully, and she paused to hope that Mom had turned the radio back on after lunch. When she got high enough, there was the screeching sound of chafed wood that suggested that the stairs might touch the floor of the attic after all . . . in which case how was she ever going to get them *closed* again? A sudden crash of depression landed on her; she'd ruined her own room, the only room in the new house that she had begun to feel a little at home in; she couldn't possibly sleep up here with this great gaping maw open virtually at the foot of her bed; and she still didn't want to move downstairs. She went on up.

There was a miniature version of the attic she'd just left at the head of the stairs, a long low narrow room. But there was no dormer window here, and the roof was so low she could not stand up straight, and the floor was only about two paces wide. But she forgot her depression, because she had found something worth finding: The tiny room was fitted out as a kind of study, with a table, or table surface, let down from one slanting wall on laths, one end nailed solidly to the beam that supported its farther end. There was a stool under it.

Annabelle drew the stool out and sat slowly down on it, feeling a little guilty, as if she were doing something she knew was not allowed. It was very hot up here, but not unbearably so, and it crossed her mind that the air was surprisingly sweet and clear for an attic; but the thought did not linger because there was too much to distract her. There were shelves running along the walls on both long sides, with a break for the table, and the shelves were awkwardly deep because of the sharpness of the roof peak. They had to run out so far toward the center for there to be space on them for books that Annabelle would have to walk sideways between them—which, she thought, sitting on the stool, was going to be a good trick, since I already have to stoop because of the ceiling. But she would have to investigate, because there were books on the shelves—books and files and boxes— boxes like the one her foot struck as she stretched her legs out; her bent knees were nearly to her chin as she sat on the stool. She pulled the box toward her, and opened it.

Small indecipherable shapes. She pointed the flashlight into the box. Small dark still-indecipherable shapes. She reached in to pick one up, her fingers touched the nearest, there was a sudden tingle that ran up her hand to her elbow; and she jerked her arm back, suddenly panting for breath and hearing her blood beating in her ears. She sat, shivering, on the stool, the box at her feet, and waited till her breath and heartbeat steadied. When she looked up again, the attic was much darker than it had been, somehow; the flashlight and the light from the stairwell had seemed plenty once she'd climbed high enough to see that she'd really found something. She had willed her eyes to adjust in eagerness, not in fear. But the shadows lay differently now, and the long thin triangular hollows behind the books on the deep shelves were . . . too black. She couldn't raise the flashlight to shine there, because she was afraid the light would not penetrate, but rebound.

Only half acknowledging what she was doing, she dropped the lid of the box shut again, picked it up, and carried it carefully down the narrow stairs—not easy, scraping her back against one side of the opening, and the arm protecting the box on the other side. Funny, there were no cobwebs, no worry of spiders in her hair, or icky dry little corpses in sticky matted spider silk; like the smell in the attic, too fresh for such a closed-up space, a strangely polite, dull-lying dust that didn't get up her nose. She set the box next to the armchair and Bridget's letter, where the sunlight struck it; it was wooden, and in the strong daylight she could see it had marks on it, though whether they were designs or letters she could not make out.

She felt a little better now, in *her* attic, Bridget's letter like a talisman and no shadows except those hiding the unswept recesses under bed and bureau; she knew what those shadows hid. And the box looked so ordinary, old and a bit splintery at the corners, two planks wide all round, with a pair of short crosspieces on each of the long sides, including bottom and lid, the size overall of a small toolbox, or four shoeboxes stacked two and two. She found herself smiling at it, for some reason; it was not a lovely object, but it looked . . . friendly.

She turned to look back at the stairs. "I would really rather have you closed, you know," she said, conversationally, aloud—and had a sudden impulse to turn back quickly and look at the box she'd brought down. She compromised, looking over her shoulder; the box was just lying there, looking as it had a moment before. She frowned at her foolishness, faced the stairs again, and, knowing it was no good but needing to make the gesture to prove it to herself, bent and seized a corner of the stairs and gave a quick heave.

They shot up into their opening so quickly she staggered and almost fell. She did let go, to catch her balance, and when she looked up, the face of the beam with the knot in it was as smooth as it had been when she had looked up at it from reading Bridget's letter. Not quite as smooth; she slid the dangling hooks back into their eyes again. She looked at the box, lying quietly and expressionlessly—why am I thinking of a box as being expressionless? she said to herself sharply—and then turned away briskly and finally, to go downstairs and out into the garden and dig. And dig and dig.

It was the best sort of distraction because there was responsibility mixed up in it. There was a lot of work still to be done on their new garden, to catch up enough this year to have some harvest at the end; and Annabelle had not merely promised to help but had effectively protested the tiny humble garden her parents had initially planned, and therefore was stuck with the result. Her mother, half pleased at the thought of fresh vegetables and half pleased at getting her daughter out of the attic on a regular basis, helped talk Dad into buying big seedlings at the nursery instead of starting from scratch with seed packets. "It's too late in the season for that," said Mom.

"But the cost!" he moaned.

"A lot cheaper than fresh vegetables at the supermarket," said Mom, a bit tartly. Her eyes met Annabelle's over the table, and both smiled. Dad was a terrible man for bargains that cost more in the end. For a moment, remembering similar past discussions, mother and daughter were in their former secure places in the family pattern, knowing where they were and why and toward what end. Or maybe only Annabelle felt the shock of a comfortable familiarity that was no longer familiar.

But some of the seedlings were still waiting to go in; after all that, Dad had bought more than they had made space for. "We'll hire you out as Rototiller Girl and earn spare cash for a thousand uses," said her father, several rows behind her, weeding in what Annabelle privately felt was a rather leisurely manner.

"How about a little red convertible for my seventeenth birthday?" said Annabelle.

"Dream on," said her father.

"How about a junker to drive to my new school this fall?" said Annabelle.

Her father was silent, and Annabelle knew she'd got it wrong. For a moment then it was almost as if the world had fallen silent too; no birds sang, and she couldn't even hear the river. Annabelle was sorry, she'd spoken without thinking, but they both knew where the unthought impulse had come from: She had gone to her old school for the last two years carpooling with some of the kids who were old enough to drive and had cars; Bill had his mother's two days a week, and Polly had one in every-other-week shares with her sister, and Sam had one almost all the time. It was too awful, thinking of having to face the humiliation of riding on a big yellow school bus with a lot of little kids as a junior in high school when she hadn't done so since she was a little kid herself.

"We'll see," her father said, surprising her. That meant maybe, and in this case it meant a pretty good maybe, because he'd know not to get her hopes up about something like this.

It was two days later she got another letter from Bill—it had only been four days since the last one—very full of himself, very full of good-guy claims of how much he missed her—"Oh, God!" she said, flinging the letter down on the floor beside her armchair. "I wish you'd get together with Sue and get it over with!" She buried her head in her hands, her loneliness an almost physical presence, listening to the silence, the silence of solitude—she lifted her head again—*too* silent. Where were the birds?

She was imagining things, of course; the birds were still singing, she could hear them again, and the sound of the wind in the apple trees. I mean, she thought, I am still hearing them. I just stopped listening for a moment, I was thinking too much about being miserable. Maybe I could stop thinking about being miserable. I'll go dig in the garden some more. The new seedlings all look happy, everything's coming up beautifully fast now, including the weeds.

A week later she got another letter from Bill, and in the same mail a letter from Susan. It had happened very suddenly, they each said in their individual ways, it had happened—in fact—the day after Bill had written last, at a party he had written about planning to go to although it wouldn't be the same without Annabelle. It was as if he and Susan had seen each other for the first time. . . . They hoped she didn't mind too much.

That evening, at supper—she hadn't told her parents about Bill; she didn't mind too much, except that she minded about everything to do with moving, and she wanted the relief to be stronger than the awful stomach-upset sense of *change* when she told them—Dad said, "I've found a junker for you." Annabelle looked up, momentarily puzzled.

"A car. You can't have forgotten already," he went on. "I asked at the garage, a day or so after you mentioned it in the garden. They've got a ten-year-old Ford that one of the mechanics' sons' girlfriends just took through high school herself and is getting a new car to go to college in. They say you don't want to drive it across country, but the mechanic's son has kept it running okay, and there's nothing wrong with it except age. Sound okay?"

Annabelle felt her face breaking into a smile, and the rest of her caught up with it almost at once. "It sounds terrific. Thanks. Thanks a lot."

"You bet, Rototiller Girl."

She'd shoved the box she'd taken down from the attic-over-the-attic into the back of her closet. (Her closet, the same shape as the rest of the room, had wonderfully deep low corner-backs, suitable for old camping gear, unfinished projects from years ago that she couldn't face throwing out or dealing with, unsorted heaps of shoes, belts, gloves, sweatshirts with spodges of paint on them from helping paint the old house two years ago when they first put it on the market, and other things that she could find an excuse for not unpacking tidily into drawers in her official bedroom downstairs, like mysterious wooden boxes.) She'd tried setting it against the wall across from her armchair, but it was such a . . . presence. She could at least pretend to ignore it when it was behind the closet door, somewhere it couldn't constantly draw her eyes.

But she kept imagining that she felt it there every time she came into the attic, and that every time she opened the closet door, it—it was like a faithful dog, she thought, hoping to be invited to jump up from its bed in the corner and go for a walk. And you always felt guilty, because you knew about the hopefulness. Sorry, she thought at it, no walks. You stay there. For now. Till I decide what to do with you. She had no desire to investigate the attic-over-the-attic further. Her first sight of it had made her think she would want to do just that: explore everything, take down every book, look in every file, find out who the secret belonged to, why, when, how. But she kept remembering the tingle up her arm—and the way the stairs had *thrown* themselves back into their gap, after all the trouble she'd had getting them down in the first place. It didn't make sense. It wasn't as if she had discovered a secret spring; the stairs were stuck, wood tight-swelled against wood, hinges that hadn't been asked to work in decades.

It's like a fairy story, she thought. Girl finds magical box in attic, all things start coming right. Boring old boyfriend takes up with someone else, stops rubbing away at her, new car—well, sort of—suddenly happens against all odds. All I need now is some friends.

The silence happened again, at once, eagerly. *No*! she yelled—silently—and there was a quiver, as of a scolded dog, and then not only was there no silence, but there never had been any silence. Sorry, she said—silently—to the . . . dog-metaphor. Sorry. I know you're . . . oh, hell! Am I losing my mind here? I can't be talking to a *box*.

That afternoon, after she finished weeding the garden, she curled up on the porch swing and started reading *The Mayor of Casterbridge*. It was the only title she recognized on the living room shelves. Dad's historical research books were all out (although not all on shelves) but not very many *reading* books. It wasn't *Lord of the Rings* (which she had read eight times), but it was easier to get into than *War and Peace* had been.

The next afternoon her father took her down to the garage to see her car, a little blue boxy thing that started as soon as she turned the key, *clunka clunka clunka*, an absolutely reliable noise, she could tell. The sort of engine noise that not only any self-respecting dog would recognize coming up the driveway, but even parents would know was you and not some stranger. "Clunker," she said, "and so I dub thee, to be mine own true, um, knight, or I suppose charger or palfrey or ambling pad."

And the day after that she drove it to Dunkin' Donuts to buy a box for her father, even though it was a Wednesday, even though family tradition said that Dunkin' Donuts, junk food in capital letters, was only a weekend splurge—and because while her father was the only admitted addict, Annabelle and her mother always somehow got through their four each too, and the boxes came home carefully arranged with everyone's favorites. Annabelle had gotten up early to do this, even knowing that her parents must hear Clunker starting up, assuming that they would assume that girl with new car can't keep herself away from it, even at six-thirty in the morning in July. Mom and Dad were only barely unsticking their eyelids over their first cups of coffee by the time she got back; she could see "weekend splurge" trying to assert itself on their faces, and failing. "Well, we had doughnuts our first day in the new house," she said. "I don't see why we shouldn't have doughnuts our first day with a new car."

"It'll give us strength for standing in line at Motor Vehicles this afternoon," Dad said, looking gloomy, but reaching for the box.

She loaded up her knapsack with library books after they returned (successfully) from the DMV and, despite the temptation to throw them in Clunker's back seat, took the walk to the library by the river, with the sun baking down on her and her back under the canvas knapsack running with sweat. As she was unloading them onto the "return" counter, she looked up and saw the girl who'd said "hi" several weeks ago, coming out of the young adult room with another girl Annabelle didn't recognize. Annabelle stiffened, but kept unloading, more slowly. She'd been catching up on the new stuff by authors she'd officially given up and privately missed—Peter Dickinson, Diana Wynne Jones, Margaret Mahy—and had *Mistress Masham's Repose* and a couple of Lang's fairy books besides. There were ten or twelve of them altogether. The girls glanced at the books, and the one who'd smiled smiled again, and again Annabelle couldn't tell if it was a friendly smile or a scornful one. But she glanced up and caught Annabelle's eye. "Hi," said Annabelle, a little too loudly. "Hi," said the girl, composedly, but the other girl was already half a step ahead, and the two of them went on, past Annabelle and out the door into the street.

Annabelle stood staring at her pile of books a moment, and then turned and went . . . not home. Back to the house she now lived in. Even Clunker sitting out front no longer cheered her. She went upstairs to her attic and began writing a letter to Bridget.

By the end of July they had peas and beans and lettuce and spinach, and basil for pesto, and dill to put on the fish they caught in the stream (Dad had asked about that at the garage, too). In August Annabelle stared at the sweet corn, willing it to grow, to not be eaten by worms and birds before the human beings got to it. She finished *The Mayor of Casterbridge* and began *Great Expectations*. Dad had disappeared into his word processor and Mom into soft sculpture orders, and unpacking was at a kind of standstill, so Annabelle had found *Great Expectations* at the library. *Tess of the D'Urbervilles* was on the shelves at home, but she didn't want to read any more Hardy, too grim, and all that landscape, it struck too near: lots of landscape, no one to talk to. Dickens was better, there was stuff to laugh at in Dickens so the sad parts were okay, you didn't feel like you were going to get lost in them.

Her favorite shoes lost a heel, tearing the leather badly in the process. "Oh, hell!" she said, looking at the mess. "I don't want to give these shoes up yet!" The silence put a nose in, questioningly, and this time she let it. The next day she drove Clunker to the next town, about half an hour from their village, and the first shoe-repair store she saw said no, past mending, but that there was this fellow at the other end of town who might do it, and he did.

"Good shoes," he said. "Worth saving. I'll have to patch that, you know; it won't be quite the same color leather, but you rub a lot of mink oil in and a little polish over and no one will know. Cost you, though. Lot of work."

"That's okay," she said. "I really like those shoes."

The sweet corn was amazing: almost no worms, and while the birds got some of it, there was so much that it didn't matter. The living room was still hedged with stacks of books and book boxes, but Mom had gotten out of the dining room and into her room upstairs, and although Annabelle managed to step on a needle and Dad a pin the first evening they tried using the dining room as a dining room, Mom, nothing daunted, invited two sets of neighbors over for dinner two days later. ("Where are the good place mats?" she shouted, an hour before their guests arrived. "I unpacked them *weeks* ago!") The Websters were about her parents' age, but their kids were Averil and Ted and Sylvia's age, and lived in California and Montana, and didn't come back East very often. The Gardners' kids were still little, seven, nine, and eleven, and although on their best behavior, a fair amount of melted butter made its way to various inappropriate places.

Everyone raved about the sweet corn. "I've never tasted anything like it, in the fifty years I've lived here," said Mr. Webster, halfway through his third ear. (He ate four, before he gave up, as did most of the grown-ups.) Annabelle went out about halfway through dinner to pick more while her mother boiled more water. "Thanks," Annabelle muttered, through her teeth, to the rows of corn, but she was speaking to a box in the attic.

When she got back in, she could hear snatches of the conversation from the dining room. "—can't seem to do anything about it. The fellows in Albany don't give a damn; one little tourist town more or less. They're much more interested in the kind of mass development that could go on all around here—more New York City bedrooms, you know."

"We're a little far out for that, surely," said Dad.

"Little you know," said Mrs. Webster. "But you don't have to care why; you do have to care that they're going to do it."

"Do what?" said Annabelle to her mother, over their hands busy husking corn.

"Highway," said her mother. "Your dad's been hearing about it—at the garage, of course—and this Mr. Webster is the head of the committee to try and stop them. He sounds like he knows what he's talking about"—this was high praise from Mom, who could tell blusterers from the real thing—"but apparently they're not getting very far. Construction is due to start this fall."

"—if you felt like it. I'd rather you didn't sue, of course, but there's no doubt that old Walker's heirs heard about the highway plans and figured they'd better scratch together some cooperation quick to realize anything at all out of the property."

"But we like it here," said Dad, and Annabelle could hear that he meant it; that it was no longer just that he and Mom had gotten a good price for the house.

"Good. Terrific. I'll send you copies of sample letters tomorrow. In fact, I'll bring them around. I suppose I don't need to tell you not to copy them straight out? Even congresspeople aren't so stupid that they don't notice—or their secretaries notice for them—the same letter coming in a hundred times. But"—and Annabelle could hear the change of tone, back to general dinner party conversation—"it's in all our interests to preserve the best cornfield in New York State." Annabelle took her cue, and carried the platter of fresh corn into the dining room.

The house was fuller of people after that—more like it had been in the old house, except these people were all grownups. Dad had always had colleagues he brought home, tweedy people with short hair, blue-jeaned people with shaggy hair. Mom had a stranger assortment of friends, from the dour brown lady who ran the local Laundromat (which Mom hadn't used since the first six months they'd lived in that town, till the washing machine went in), whose thick East Indian accent baby Annabelle was the first to understand, to various arts and crafts types, some of whom showed up clinking with beaded hair and bracelets and talked about auras and past lives. Now they had political activists—polite political activists, with neat hair and polo shirts, but with the gleam in the eye and the edge to the voice that told you what they really were.

Annabelle painted a few posters and stuffed some envelopes, but as much as she was growing to love her riverside walk, she could not persuade herself that she cared enough to get really involved. It wasn't that she still hoped that if things didn't work out here, they could go back to their old lives; they couldn't. The new people were in their old house—Bridget said they had repapered most of the downstairs, and taken out the old mock chandelier in the living room and put in track lighting—you didn't get to go back. Annabelle knew that. Maybe if there had been some kids her own age involved in this highway thing; there probably were; but she didn't know where they were or what they did, and she was too—proud? discouraged? alienated?—to go to the effort of asking.

She knew her parents were worrying about her, but she also knew that so long as she didn't make a show of being disoriented or unhappy, they would leave her alone a while longer. So she went on taking care of the garden, and going to the library, and ignoring the implications of the box in the closet that she believed she didn't really believe in, and smiling occasionally even if she didn't mean it. Enough to keep her parents from doing anything about worrying about her.

By the end of August only Bridget was writing to her regularly any more. Annabelle wrote back, but found it hard to have anything to say; weeding the garden wasn't very interesting, or actually it was interesting, the feel of earth on your hands, dirt under your fingernails, the surprising satisfaction every time a weed came up with that tiny *rip* that told you you got the roots and not just pulled the top off, the heat, the sun, the bugs, the occasional whiff of cool river—but it didn't go in a letter very well. It was what kept Annabelle going, but it wasn't anything she could talk about. This seemed to be part of not having anyone to talk to. It was very confusing. It was as if she were forgetting something vital. And so she spent more and more of her time in the garden, where talking was superfluous. She finished *Great Expectations* and began *Barchester Towers*.

School was starting in two weeks. The shops all had BACK TO SCHOOL SALE banners in their windows. She stopped herself from wishing for the perfect winter coat, half out of a feeling that Clunker—and the corn, and her shoes—were enough, half out of not being sure she wanted to know what her perfect winter coat really was—and a spare half being angry with herself for thinking consciously about the whole thing. The box in the closet was just an old box full of junk. That's all. It was her imagination that her closet felt wistful. That she could taste it, like a mist, when she opened the closet door. That it tasted like an old sadness sweeping back in after new hope.

But the sense of old sadness stayed with her, till she began to feel that it was her own, that it was not that she had left her friends and the shape of her life behind in her old town, but that she had always felt out of place and lonely, and that she was . . . old, old. That she had felt this way for a long, long time. She had a nightmare, ten days before the first day of school, in which she looked in her mirror and her hair was grey, and she was squinting through thick glasses—one battered earpiece was held in place by a bit of twisted wire—and she stared at herself, knowing she'd done nothing with her life, knowing that she'd given up. . . . She sat bolt upright, gasping. It was morning; in fact she'd overslept. She'd had a nightmare because she'd overslept, and because school was starting, and she was afraid to go to this new school.

She got up and dressed, and went outdoors. But even the garden held no peace for her today, and she went on down to the restless river, and turned right, away from the town, and then turned again and retraced her footsteps, stepped over the low wall, and wandered down the main street. It was late enough now that the shops were opening and there were people on the streets; she knew a few to say hello to from her parents' NO HIGHWAY HERE group, and one young mother surprised her by asking if she'd like to baby-sit. Annabelle remembered her; she had one of those really passionate voices, and her posters were better than anyone else's. Annabelle, with an armful of delightedly thrashing two-year-old, said, "Oh—sure. I guess." She'd liked baby-sitting, back in her old life; she'd found the self-absorption of little kids a kick, and had a good time with them—so long as their mothers came home again after a few hours and rescued her.

She walked on, feeling a new little sense of warmth: something she could do besides hoe and read. Something to do with people, something she understood, changing diapers and keeping little hands away from stoves and closing doors—unlike writing bold angry words she didn't believe on pieces of paper to be looked at by government officials she couldn't imagine about the fate of a town she was a stranger to.

She went to the library and into the young adults' room and, without thinking, found herself in front of the *L*'s. The *Orange Fairy Book* was in; she'd been waiting for that one, before she started *The Mayor of Casterbridge*. She pulled it down and stood looking at it. It wouldn't hurt, reading another book of fairy tales. What was she afraid of? She was staring down at the book in her hands and not paying attention to her feet, which had begun moving again; and then the sudden sunlight startled her as she came out from the shelves into the muddle of rec room chairs. She stopped.

There were only four of them this time. She could feel her face freeze again, but behind the frozenness she felt the longing: someone to talk to, a friend. A friend. And just as suddenly the silence was hovering. *Please*, it said. And they stood there, she and it, and the four kids looked at the one kid, and Annabelle looked back.

No, she said to the silence. I'm sorry. But not this. And it went away from her, and she felt the old sadness draw back too; she knew, clearly, at least for that moment, what was hers and what was not. And with that knowledge came a sudden rush of confidence. She stepped forward. "Hi," she said. "My name's Annabelle."

"Yeah," said one of the boys. "We know. I'm Alan. My older sister Nancy's on that NO HIGHWAY HERE committee. I'm sorry I missed the corn, though."

"There's more," said Annabelle. "All you have to do is stuff a few envelopes and hang around looking hungry. My mom likes feeding people."

"My mom too," said one of the girls. "Everybody but her

family." There was a ripple of laughter—this was obviously an old joke—excluding Annabelle, who suddenly wondered if she should have said what she did, so quickly, and to a boy too.

But before her little bubble of confidence burst into nothing, the other girl spoke over the end of the laughter: "You're reading Andrew Lang." It was the girl Annabelle had seen twice before, the one who'd smiled.

"Oh . . . I . . ." began Annabelle, floundering, but the girl went on: "I love the old Lang books, and *Wind in the Willows* and *The Borrowers* and stuff. I saw you that day in the library bringing back all my favorites, but Mary was in a hurry or I would have said something. I'm Nell."

"Nell's gonna be a writer," drawled Alan. Nell scowled.

"When we were all in fourth grade, Nell wrote a story about a lavender unicorn that sucked nectar out of flowers with its horn, like a bee, you know, and Alan stole it and we all read it," said the girl who had spoken first.

"And I've *never* forgiven you," said Nell.

"She has a word processor now, the stuff's harder to steal," said Alan, unrepentant.

"You're starting school with us in a week, aren't you?" said Nell.

"Yes," said Annabelle in a voice much smaller than she'd have liked.

"You'll be glad to get out of your house, I think," said the girl who had the mother who liked to feed everyone but her family, "now that NO HIGHWAY HERE has taken it over."

"Yeah, well, I'm glad somebody's doing something," said the other boy, who had been silent till now.

"So am I," said Nell.

"Lavender unicorns for peace," murmured Alan.

"Let's get out of here before some librarian comes and snarls at us," said the second boy.

"If they didn't want anybody to sit around here talking, why did they set it up to look like a place where you can sit around and talk?" said Nell, reasonably, but she got up. "You busy?" she said to Annabelle. "We'll probably go over to the Good Baker. You can sit there forever for the price of a cup of coffee."

"Sure," said Annabelle.

"Say, you have a car, don't you?" said Alan. "You bought Pat's old clunker."

"That's right," said Annabelle.

"Be careful," said Nell. "Alan's an opportunist. Alan O. Poole, that's him. You've already invited him to dinner, although you may not be aware of it."

"I have a car," said Alan, with dignity, as they threaded their way through the shelves.

"You have a chassis on four wheels," said the other girl. "There's a difference."

"Hush," said Nell, and they went through the library lobby, where the one librarian on duty looked at them warily over her spectacles.

Annabelle went home in the late afternoon, her mind in a whirl. She knew she liked Nell—besides the fact she almost had to like anyone who would admit in public that she still reread *The Borrowers* the summer before her junior year of high school—and she thought she liked Diana, the other girl. Alan was cute, but he knew it, which Annabelle didn't like, but Nell seemed to think he was a good guy anyway. The other boy, Frank, seemed to see the worst sides of things— but she kind of understood that, and it wasn't as if he was making any of it up or anything. He was the one who told her more about NO HIGHWAY HERE; she supposed she'd heard it before, in snatches, at least, at home, but it was different when someone was explaining it specifically to you, and telling you in such a way that you believed that it was important to him that you paid attention and understood.

For the first time there was a tiny thread of feeling under her breastbone that said: It would be a pity if the highway came here. If six lanes of hot noisy tarmac crossed just behind the main street, if it cut down all the trees along the river for half a mile, if those meadows and farmers' fields—even if the farmers were reimbursed, which they were supposed to be—were ruined forever as meadows and farm fields. If all those rabbits and skunks and raccoons and porcupines—even grey squirrels, and she didn't like grey squirrels—went homeless. And if the air, even at midnight, smelled faintly of exhaust. No. She didn't want the highway here either. Even if she left this place the day after she got her high school diploma and never came back.

She lay awake a long time that night, watching the moon through her window, turning on her side to keep it in view for as long as possible. She was meeting Nell and Diana and Mary, whom Annabelle had seen the once several weeks ago, the day after tomorrow. They were going shopping for winter coats, and anything else they might see.

And a few days after that was the town meeting. Nell and Alan were going, and some of their friends she hadn't met yet, Linda and George and Kate and some other names she'd forgotten, and Annabelle was thinking about going with them. Then Frank telephoned her that afternoon and asked if she was coming. Of course, she found herself saying, and then Frank said, "Um, well, I'll look for you there, you know I could tell you who everybody was and stuff. You know, the businessmen who think it would be a good idea, and the green guys who know better."

Frank was short, no taller than Annabelle, and he walked funny, kind of crouched and tense. Nothing like Bill. "Sure," said Annabelle. "Sounds great."

Her elation lasted till about halfway through the meeting, when it became obvious to everyone that NO HIGHWAY HERE was losing. The people on the other side were smoother, and they knew how to talk about "helping the economic profile of this rather depressed area." They made the highway sound like a slight inconvenience for a good cause—what were a few meadows and trees one way or another? It wasn't as if this town didn't have lots of meadows and trees. In fact, that was its whole problem, that it didn't have much else but meadows and trees, and small family farms, well, everyone knew what was happening to small family farms all over the country these days. Local farmers hereabouts were lucky the highway people were interested. When a few of the NO HIGHWAY HERE people began to get angry, they only looked silly. Even Mr. Webster's facts and statistics—read out as gravely as anyone could read—didn't make enough of an impression. Not as much of an impression as the sleek leather briefcases and designer three-piece suits of the fellows who murmured the magic word *jobs*.

Annabelle lay awake that night too, but she was restless and irritable. Why can't anything be simple? she thought. Why did my parents have to decide that this was the small town they wanted to move to? Why did I decide to get involved anyway? Who cares? Who needs friends anyway? But she knew better, and the anger drained out of her. Where she was was here, and what she was was involved. She did care. It had happened. And now they were going to get a

189

highway. Her parents had trailed home as silent and depressed as the kids; that was how she knew. If Mr. Webster had said anything to them afterward to give them hope, they would have been grim but not oppressed. Not silent and exhausted, the way they were.

And then she thought of the box in her closet. She'd been unaware of it since the afternoon in the library when she'd met Nell and the rest. No wonder, she thought, it was all your imagination anyway, you just made something up to keep yourself from being quite so lonely, like a little kid makes up an imaginary friend. I should have named it, she thought. Bess. Or Song of the Wind, or something: a kind of lavender-unicorn name. Well, I'm glad I didn't give up about my shoes without trying, even if I tried for the wrong reasons.

She turned over and tried to go to sleep—school was only two days away now, but she thought of it with a much pleasanter sense of alarmed anticipation than she had done a week ago—but sleep refused to come. Instead she fell into what she assumed must be a kind of waking dream: She was dreaming about the box in the closet. I have something for you, she told it. But I'll need help. Can you get Clunker to start silently, just once?

She sat up. Nonsense! she said to herself. I'm *awake*! But she got out of bed anyway, and went to her closet. She could see the cracks around the door, because they were . . . not quite dark. She opened the door, cautiously. The light was very faint, and grey, almost furtive: pleading. It was the marks on the box that were glowing, almost like tiny crooked windows with the end of twilight coming through. Or the beginnings of dawn. Okay, she murmured. We'll try.

She put her clothes on, tucked the box under one arm, and

crept downstairs. I'll know in a minute, she thought. When I try to start Clunker. But what am I going to tell my parents if they see me in the driver's seat at two in the morning with a box with funny-looking marks which may or may not be glowing on it in the passenger seat beside me? She turned the key, and Clunker started at once, as it always did; but with a kind of low purring hum, so faint she could barely hear it, and knew the engine was running only by the vibration through her feet. She put it in gear, and they rolled gently down the driveway.

I'm sure there's a right way to do this, she said to the box, but I don't know what it is. She drove in a wide, ragged circle, depending on what roads there were, and which ones she recognized, all around the town. And every now and then, when she felt that she'd been driving long enough, she stopped, and opened the box, reached in till she touched something, picked it up—all the things were smallish, hand-sized, lumpy, roundish, and very faintly warm to the touch—carried it to the roadside, scrabbled a little in the earth with a screwdriver out of Clunker's glove compartment, put it in, covered it over, said, "Thanks," out loud, and went back to the car. The first time she'd put her hand in the box she'd hesitated, remembering that eerie tingle; but nothing of the sort happened this time, except a curious kind of contentment in the touch of the thing against her palm, a sense of cradling, as you might do with a kitten. She remembered a description she'd read somewhere of one of those breeds of hairless cat; the journalist said that she'd thought they were really ugly, but then had held a kitten in her hand, and thought better of her first reaction. It felt like a warm peach, she wrote. The things out of the box were a bit like faintly knobbly warm peaches.

It took her several hours. She was settling the last one under leaf mold when she suddenly thought: I have one more favor to ask you. The attic-over-the-attic: Could it no longer be there? Somehow. I mean, if there's more of you up there, I don't want to have to deal with it. I'm an ordinary girl, you know. I want to go on being ordinary.

And she heard the silence for the last time.

When the new superhighway went in, there was a great round bow in its elegant engineered sweep north and west: a very odd-looking, out-of-place bow, shaped a little like the way grains of wood spread out and then curl in around a knot, giving wide berth to a tiny town of about five thousand people out in the middle of nowhere. The town was beautifully centered in the bow, so beautifully that even an engineer had to admire it, however badly it twisted the handsome strong lay of the highway. The ecological reports, everyone said vaguely. Something about the ecology of the area. Don't really know; somebody must have had an in somewhere. There isn't really any reason at all.